Show You No Mercy 3

Vendetta

K. Powell

Authentic Reads Publication

Copyright © 2024 by Authentic Reads Publications.

All rights reserved.

No part of this publication may be reproduced, distributed, or transmitted in any form or by any means, including photocopying, recording, or other electronic or mechanical methods, without the prior written permission of the publisher, except as permitted by U.S. copyright law. For permission requests, contact [include publisher/author contact info].

The story, all names, characters, and incidents portrayed in this production are fictitious. No identification with actual persons (living or deceased), places, buildings, and products is intended or should be inferred.

Book Cover by Black Girl Digital Labs

ISBN: 979-8-9869925-4-9 (Paperback)

ISBN: 979-8-9869925-5-6 (EBook)

To those who have walked the fine line between vengeance
and forgiveness,
To the souls who have found strength in their darkest
moments,
And to every reader who has felt the weight of a vendetta in
their heart,
This final chapter is for you.

AUTHENTIC READS PUBLICATION

SHOW YOU NO MERCY 3

VENDETTA

K. POWELL

Revenge isn't a show of strength; it's the mirror that reflects our most fragile scars.

Chapter 1

Gambling with Fate

The casino was buzzing, alive with the sound of winning and losing, a constant back-and-forth of hope and disappointment. Luke was at the heart of it all, nodding to regulars and checking in with his staff. Despite the smiles and the casual chats, his eyes kept darting to the exits. It was a habit he couldn't shake, a sign of the unease that sat heavy in his gut.

He tried to keep his breathing steady, not to let on how on edge he really was. The weight of running this place was nothing compared to the weight of the unknown, of waiting for the other shoe to drop.

As he made his rounds, his gaze lifted to the balcony. Nora was there, leaning on the railing, watching him. Her hand lifted slightly, a silent call. He made his way through the crowd and up the stairs, his heart pounding a little harder with each step.

In the quiet of his office, Nora's hand on the door sounded loud to him. "You need to calm down," she said. Her voice was firm but kind.

"How can I? It's been too quiet since Veronica's call. Six months with no word from her, that's not good," Luke said. The words rushed out of him like they'd been waiting just behind his lips.

Nora sighed. "Maybe she had a change of heart. Not everyone holds a grudge forever."

But Luke was already shaking his head, pacing the small space. "You don't know her like I do. Silence from Veronica isn't peace—it's her planning her next move."

Nora stepped closer and put her hands on his arms. "Stop worrying about Veronica for a second," she said, her thumbs rubbing circles over his skin. "We still have to break the news to my family."

The mention of the family brought him back to the here and now, to the casino that buzzed below them and the life they were trying to rebuild, one that was always one step away from falling apart again if Veronica had her way.

Nora turned her left hand around, the light catching on her engagement ring. It was an emerald cut stargaze ring, the main diamond large and clear, set in a band of platinum. Small diamonds encrusted the band, twinkling like stars around the central gem that seemed to hold a universe of its own. It was elegant and bold, much like Nora herself.

Luke couldn't help but smile every time he saw that ring. "What do you think Avery and Sage are going to say?" he asked.

She wrapped her arms around his neck, and her eyes shined almost as much as the ring. "Avery will be thrilled. She adores you. But Sage, well, you know how she is. She thinks you're too young for me and that it's all moving too fast."

Their tender moment was suddenly broken by Benjamin, the casino's accountant. His face wore a mix of concern and urgency as he approached. "Sorry to interrupt, but we have a problem," he said, placing a stack of documents on Luke's desk.

Luke glanced down at the papers, filled with numbers and terms that might as well have been another language. "What am I looking at here?" he asked, the confusion apparent in his furrowed brow and the slight squint of his eyes.

Benjamin leaned forward, his expression serious. "I was reviewing our latest financial reports, and there are discrepancies between what the casino should be making and what is actually being deposited."

Luke took a deep breath and rubbed his forehead. At 26, running a whole casino was daunting, and his face showed it—all worry lines and puzzled eyes, a young man suddenly feeling the weight of his responsibilities.

"So you telling me the money ain't adding up?" Nora asked, her tone sharp with concern.

"Exactly," Benjamin confirmed, nodding.

Nora reached for the documents, scanning them with a critical eye. "How do we know these aren't just accidents?"

"It's been happening too consistently to be an accident," Benjamin said, his voice firm. "Someone is intentionally skimming profits."

Luke shot up from his seat, a surge of adrenaline fueling his decision. "We need to call a meeting right now. Get everyone in."

Nora's hand on his shoulder was calming and grounding. "Let's not rush into accusations," she advised. "We should increase our surveillance quietly. We need to catch whoever's doing this without tipping them off."

Benjamin nodded in agreement. "I will keep an extra close watch on the financials and any irregularities, and you'll be the first to know." With that assurance, he left the office, closing the door softly behind him.

Left alone with Nora, Luke's face was a picture of vulnerability, his usual confidence replaced with uncertainty. "What am I going to do?" he asked, his eyes wide and searching like a puppy seeking guidance.

Nora's expression softened, her resolve clear as she held his gaze. "I got you," she said, her voice a blend of reassurance and strength. "No one is going to tear us down."

Chapter 2

Unexpected Encounters

The high school's front steps were a whirlwind of activity as the final bell rang. Students poured out of the building, their laughter and shouts filling the air with the electric buzz of freedom. Sage and Tegan leaned against the school's iron fence, standing quietly in the middle of all the typical high school chaos.

Tegan flipped her hair back and turned to Sage with a teasing glint in her eye. "So, what'd you score on the math test?"

Sage thumbed through her phone. "85, I was aiming for a perfect score," she replied, her voice tinged with disappointment.

Tegan laughed, nudging Sage playfully. "Girl, please, an 85 is passing, and you're stressing over nothing."

But Sage's brow was furrowed, and her gaze drifted off to the basketball courts in the distance. "It's not just about passing," she said, her voice tightened. "I need to graduate early. I've got so much to catch up on, what with the extra classes I'm taking and..." Her eyes flicked back to the courts, where the girl's team was practicing, their movements a reminder of what she was missing. "... and I need to get back on the basketball team."

The determination in her stance and the way she clutched her phone a bit too tightly spoke volumes. It was clear that for Sage, this wasn't just about grades or sports; it was about reclaiming a part of her life that she thought she lost.

"Graduate early? Why would you want to rush through school?" Tegan asked, her brow creased in genuine curiosity.

Sage was about to respond when her attention snapped to the school doors. Cylus was making his way out, his backpack slung casually over one shoulder. Tegan caught the shift in Sage's focus and leaned in, and her voice dropped to a whisper. "Or is it about graduating early for Cylus?"

Sage shot her a playful glare but didn't reply. Her face lit up as she approached Cylus, her arms reaching out to encircle his neck in a warm embrace. "Hey, babe," she greeted.

Cylus returned the embrace, planting a soft kiss on her lips. "What's up?" His smile didn't quite reach his eyes, hinting at some underlying concern.

"You okay?" Sage asked, her eyes searched his face for clues.

He brushed off her concern with a shrug, though his smile remained unconvincing. "I'm good, don't worry about me," he insisted.

The trio fell into a casual conversation; their laughter punctuated the air. But their joy was short-lived. A black Cadillac Escalade with tinted windows cruised by, its presence looming and ominous. It moved slowly, almost teasingly, as if considering a stop right in front of them.

Sage felt a knot tighten in her stomach, and her breath caught in her throat. The vehicle eventually moved on, but the sense of relief that followed was evident. As the car disappeared from view, Sage finally exhaled; the breath she hadn't realized she was holding escaped in a rush.

Tegan's voice sliced through the lingering silence, "Who the hell was that?" Her eyes followed the disappearing car; a frown creased her forehead.

Sage, still caught in the moment, felt a hard lump form in her throat. She turned her gaze away from the receding tail lights, staring blankly into the distance. Her mind raced with possibilities, each more unsettling than the last. Who could be inside such a car, and why did it feel like they were being watched? Sage knew the streets around their school often held surprises, but this felt different. This was personal.

***

Sage sat in the circle of chairs, glancing around at the other teens gathered in the room. The soft hum of the fluorescent lights above was the only sound as everyone waited for the session to begin. The walls were adorned with motivational posters, and a faint scent of lavender filled the air, meant to create a calming atmosphere. The room was a stark contrast to the chaos of her recent life, a small sanctuary where healing could begin.

The sign on the door read "New Horizons Teen Recovery," a name meant to inspire hope and a fresh start. Sage had been attending these meetings for a few weeks now, trying to get a handle on her addiction to cocaine. It had been a dark chapter in her life, one she was determined to close.

The group leader, a kind woman named Ms. Rivera, entered the room with a warm smile. Her presence was comforting, her eyes filled with empathy and understanding. She took a seat and looked around the circle, acknowledging each teen with a nod.

"Welcome back, everyone," Ms. Rivera began, her voice gentle yet firm. "Today, we're going to talk about coping mechanisms. How do we deal with the stress and triggers that push us towards substance use?"

Sage shifted in her seat, her hands clasped tightly in her lap. She listened as a few others shared their stories, each one a reminder that she wasn't alone in her struggle. When it was her turn, she took a deep breath and began to speak.

"I used to think cocaine was the only thing that could help me deal with my problems," Sage admitted, her voice shaky. "But being here, I've realized that there are other ways to cope. It's not easy, but I'm trying."

Ms. Rivera nodded encouragingly. "That's a great step, Sage. Can you share some of the strategies you've learned?"

Sage thought for a moment, then nodded. "I've started writing in a journal. It helps me get my thoughts out without turning to drugs. And I've been spending more time with my family. They've been through a lot, too, and it helps to support each other."

The other teens nodded in agreement, and a few shared their own coping mechanisms. As the session continued, Sage felt a growing sense of hope. It wasn't going to be easy, but she was starting to see a path forward.

After the meeting, Sage lingered near the coffee machine, her fingers nervously tapping against the plastic cup she held. She watched as the other teens began to disperse, but a few stayed behind, forming small groups to chat. She took a deep breath, mustering the courage to approach a nearby cluster of teens.

"Hey, Sage," a girl with curly hair and bright green eyes said, offering a friendly smile. "How are you feeling?"

Sage returned the smile, feeling a bit more at ease. "I'm okay, Emily. Just trying to take it one day at a time."

Emily nodded, her expression understanding. "I get that. Every day is a new challenge, but we're in this together."

A boy with shaggy brown hair and a shy demeanor joined the conversation. "Yeah, Sage, you're not alone. We've all been there. If you ever need to talk or just hang out, we're here for you."

Sage felt a warmth spread through her chest. "Thanks, Alex. That means a lot."

Another girl, petite with short-cropped hair and a nose ring, chimed in. "We should exchange numbers, you know, to keep each other accountable. Sometimes just having someone to text when things get tough can make a big difference."

Sage nodded enthusiastically. "That sounds like a great idea, Jenna."

They all pulled out their phones, quickly exchanging numbers and adding each other to a group chat they humorously named "Sober Crew." Sage felt a sense of belonging that she hadn't felt in a long time.

"Hey, why don't we grab coffee sometime?" Emily suggested. "We can talk about anything except drugs and therapy. Just normal stuff."

Sage's smile widened. "I like that it would be nice to have some normalcy."

Alex grinned, his shyness melting away. "Awesome, we can meet at that café downtown. They have the best muffins."

Jenna laughed. "And the worst coffee, but I'm in."

As they wrapped up their conversation, Sage felt a newfound sense of hope. She wasn't just attending meetings; she was building a support network, making friends who understood her struggles and wanted to help her succeed. Little did she know, the real danger was lurking, waiting for the perfect moment to strike.

Chapter 3

Family Secrets

The air was filled with the scent of lavender as sunlight streamed through the blinds, casting a warm glow in the room. Sarah, holding baby Laverne in her arms, smiled broadly as she made playful baby noises, entertaining her little one. Laverne's giggles filled the space, a sound of pure joy.

Mylan, busy cooking in the kitchen, paused to watch his wife and daughter. A smile touched his lips as he observed the tender scene. He watched for a moment longer, then turned back to his cooking, the familiar sounds of the kitchen blending with the laughter of his family.

In their home, away from the outside world, these simple moments of family life were cherished. It was a brief, peaceful rest that differed from the uncertainties that lay beyond their doorstep.

"Baby, look at Lala, she's smiling," Sarah called out to Mylan, her eyes sparkling with joy as she watched their daughter. "This is everything."

Mylan, wiping his hands on a cloth, looked over and smiled. "What's everything?" he asked with a playful tone.

"You, me, Lala, our family," Sarah replied, her voice filled with warmth. "This life we're building together, away from all the illegal stuff and family drama. It's just us, and that's all I ever wanted, just us, forever."

Mylan's expression shifted; a touch of guilt fleeted across his face as a frown settled in. "About that," he muttered, his voice low.

Sarah's heart sank slightly. She gently placed Laverne in her bassinet, her movements slow and deliberate. Mylan pulled up a chair, sitting down in front of her with a serious look.

"I'm still working for Adonis," he confessed.

Sarah's eyes widened. "You promised me, Mylan, that after the baby arrived, you would leave that world behind."

"Adonis Weston isn't the kind of man you just walk away from," Mylan said, his tone defensive yet weary. "And the money I make... it's enough for all of us. You wouldn't need to go back to work. I've got you covered."

Sarah stood abruptly, her frustration evident as she began to pace the room. "I didn't spend years in nursing school to end up a housewife, and you know I'm studying to be a Neurologist," she said, her voice tinged with anger. "And what am I supposed to tell my parents? That my husband, whom they've never met, is a gun trafficker? They're already upset I got married and had a baby without them meeting you. This just makes everything so much more complicated."

Mylan's face hardened slightly. "As far as your parents are concerned, you can tell them I'm a train conductor or make some shit up," he insisted.

Sarah let out a sound of frustration, her patience wearing thin. "Mylan, my dad is Max Langford. He's the freaking captain of a police unit, and he doesn't trust anyone. The only reason you're not on his radar is because you've managed to stay out of jail."

Mylan turned to her with a wry smile, kissing her cheek before heading back to the kitchen. "That's because I'm good at what I do. I never get caught."

Sarah checked on Laverne, finding her sound asleep, then followed Mylan. Her voice was heavy with worry. "I can't do this, and I won't bury my husband. This isn't the life I want for us or Laverne."

Mylan paused and wiped his hands on his sweats. "You knew what this was when you met me. For god sake, baby, you met me in the hospital after I got shot. Did you think that I was a law-abiding citizen? Even after I told you what I did for a living, you stayed and married me. Why is it a problem now?"

She motioned towards Laverne. "Now that she's here, who knows what's next? Between you and your sister, we could be endangering our daughter. Can't you see that?"

Mylan took a deep breath and held her hand, his eyes meeting hers earnestly. "Laverne will never be in danger, not as long as I'm around, and neither will you. I'll start slowing things down, and maybe I can even get a job at the casino with Nora. She owes me a favor," he added with a hopeful smile.

Sarah managed a half-smile in return, but the worry in her eyes didn't fade. She wanted to believe him, to trust that their little family could find a way out of the shadows that his life cast over them.

***

The graveyard was a quiet, solemn place. Rows of tombstones stood like silent sentinels under the watchful eyes of old, stoic trees. Warren walked slowly through the aisles, his footsteps muffled by the lush, manicured grass. He stopped at one particular grave, its tombstone more familiar than any other.

The stone read 'Donny Lafayette,' followed by his birth and death dates. Below, an inscription called him 'A Beloved

Son, a Loyal Friend,' and in a final, heartfelt addition, 'A Light Extinguished Too Soon.' The words hit hard, reminding him of everything he had lost.

Warren sat on the grass in front of the tombstone, his gaze fixed intensely on the engraved letters. He opened his mouth as if to speak, but the words escaped him. His hand clutched an object tightly – a graduation cap with its tassel dangling off the side. Gently, he placed it on top of the tombstone.

"Congratulations," he whispered, his voice barely audible. The tassel swayed slightly in the breeze as if acknowledging his gesture. In that quiet, hallowed space, surrounded by memories and what-ifs, Warren allowed himself to remember, grieve, and reflect on the journey that had brought him here.

Warren's voice broke as he tried to speak. "I'm..." He cleared his throat, struggling for composure. "I'm sorry," he finally managed, his head bowing under the weight of his words. "Sorry, it took me so long to come see you." A pause hung in the air as he gathered his thoughts. "I just... I didn't know what to say."

His eyes closed tightly, and a single tear traced down his cheek. In a choked whisper, he said, "This is all my fault. It should've been me, not you. All you ever wanted was to party and flirt with girls." He let out a bitter laugh at the memory, and then silence fell again.

Taking a deep breath, Warren wiped the tears from his face. "Sometimes I wonder how things would've turned out if I hadn't gone to Mikey's that night. Maybe I'd be a big-time basketball player by now. And you... you would've been right there with me, cheering me on."

Warren's confession felt like a lament and a fragile bridge to a past that was forever out of reach.

"I was supposed to be the one looking out for you," Warren continued, his voice thick with remorse. He clenched his jaw, and a hardened resolve replaced the tears that had once threatened to overflow. His eyes, now dry, burned with anger. "I'm your big cousin, and I failed to protect you. But I won't fail in getting you justice."

He rose to his feet, his posture rigid with newfound resolve. "If that means someone has to get hurt, then so be it." The words were more than a vow; they were a solemn oath, spoken to the silent gravestones that bore witness to his promise.

Chapter 4

Tension

Nora waited in line, her gaze fixed ahead as she slowly inched towards the front desk. The correctional facility was a stark, unwelcoming place; its walls echoed with the muted sounds of a world locked away from freedom. When she finally reached the front, a uniformed officer looked up, his expression impassive. "ID, please," he requested in a flat, procedural tone.

After Nora presented her identification, she passed the rigorous security checks, where they briefly checked her belongings. Then, they escorted her through a series of bleak, brightly lit corridors. She arrived in a large room filled with round tables, each one a designated spot for visitors to meet with inmates.

An officer gestured towards a table near the center of the room. "Please sit here," he instructed. Nora took her seat, feeling the oppressive atmosphere of the place. Around her, other visitors and inmates were engaged in quiet conversations.

Nora waited, preparing herself for this forthcoming meeting, a conversation that was likely to be anything but ordinary.

Nora's breath caught as she watched an officer escort an inmate into the room. The woman, with a slight smirk on her lips, walked with a certain air of defiance. Their eyes locked instantly, holding a depth of unspoken words.

As the woman sat across from Nora, the officer lingered momentarily before leaving them to their private conversation. The silence stretched between them, charged with anticipation.

Finally, she spoke, "They told me I had a visitor. Never would've guessed it'd be you, Nora. Especially since you're the reason I'm in here," Kamari said, her words heavy with a mix of sarcasm and bitterness.

Nora leaned forward, her voice steady but sincere. "I came here to check on you, see how you're doing."

Kamari scoffed, a hint of scorn in her laughter. "Bitch, I'm in jail. How the hell you think I'm doing?" Her eyes narrowed as she leaned in, closing the space between them. "You ain't here for me. You're just scared about my trial coming up. Scared, I'll spill about Sage and what went down with Que."

Nora tried to keep her composure. "What happened was messed up, but we're still family, Kamari."

"Family?" Kamari's voice rose in disbelief, her fist hitting the metal table with a clang that echoed in the sterile room. "Were we 'family' when you shot my dad right in front of me?"

"Our dad," Nora interjected softly.

Kamari's laugh was bitter. "Oh, now he's 'our' dad? Girl, please. You left him to die. He bled out right in my arms, and I was just five years old."

Nora opened her mouth to respond, but Kamari was on a roll. "Don't come in here playin' the big sis card. That ship sailed 17 years ago."

"I told you I'd be there for you through all this shit. And I'm here, ain't I?" Nora said with frustration.

Kamari leaned back, distancing herself from Nora. Her expression hardened. "You think I bought any of that bull you said? You ain't nothin' but a liar." She crossed her arms over her chest defiantly. "I wanna see Sage."

Nora shook her head firmly. "Hell no. I'm not dragging my daughter into this mess. She's finally doing good in school, and I'm not letting her get sidetracked by all of this." She gestured around the bleak visiting room.

The air between them crackled with tension as Kamari's lips twisted into a sly smirk, eyes glinting with a cold, calculated look. "Here's how it's gonna go down. Sage comes to see me, or I start dropping names." The threat in her voice was unmistakable.

Nora rose to her feet, her movement quick but controlled. She straightened her blouse to regain her composure. "I'll see what I can do," she said through gritted teeth.

Kamari rose, leaning forward, her palms flat on the dusty table. She locked eyes with Nora, her gaze intense. "Don't 'see,' Nora. Just do it!"

***

Sunday dinner at Mylan and Sarah's condo was a lively affair. The table was packed, with Nora sitting between Avery and Sage. Mylan and Sarah, each at one end of the table. Laughter and conversation flowed freely among them. Luke, seated next to Sage, added to the cheerful atmosphere. The room was filled with the comforting smells of the meal cooked by Mylan. It was a moment when everyone seemed to leave their worries at the door, simply enjoying the presence of family.

Nora gently tapped her wine glass with a knife, catching everyone's attention. Standing up, she smiled warmly at the gathering. "I just want to express how happy I am that we're all here together. The past few years have been... well, hell, to put it mildly." Her eyes briefly met Avery's and Sage's. "I'm especially grateful for my girls and their forgiveness. It means the world to me."

Luke cut in as Avery and Sage were about to raise their glasses, his Italian accent lending a unique cadence to his words. "I gotta say, being the new guy here, I appreciate how you've all welcomed me into the family," he said with a genuine smile.

He gently took Nora's hand, leading her to his side of the table, where they both faced the family. A buzz of curiosity filled the air. "Nora and I have something important to share with you all," Luke announced, pausing to exchange a meaningful glance with Nora. They stood united, ready to share their news with the family.

"We're engaged," Nora announced, her voice steady yet filled with emotion. She reached into her pocket, pulling out a ring that shined in the room's soft light. With a graceful motion, she slid the ring onto her finger, its sparkle catching everyone's eyes.

A hush fell over the room, a blanket of silence that spoke volumes. They fixed their gaze on the couple, their faces etched with surprise and disbelief.

The age difference between Nora and Luke, him being ten years younger, added an extra layer of astonishment to the moment.

Nora and Luke stood there, hand in hand, the ring on her finger a symbol of their commitment, unmoved by the quiet shock that had momentarily gripped the room.

Sarah was the first to break the silence, her voice brimmed with excitement. "Oh my god! Congratulations!" She quickly got up and embraced Luke and Nora in a warm, heartfelt hug.

Meanwhile, Avery, Sage, and Mylan shared a look of mutual surprise. The news had caught them off guard. Mylan voiced the thoughts that seemed to linger in the air: "This is unexpected. Why so soon? Y'all haven't even been together that long, right? It hasn't even been a year."

His words reflected his concern as the family processed the sudden announcement.

Nora's eyes narrowed as she turned to face Mylan, with defensiveness in her tone. "Mylan, what's your problem?" she asked her question laced with irritation at his response.

Mylan's frustration was evident as he gestured towards Avery and Sage. "My problem is, you've just started fixing things with them," he pointed out, his voice rising slightly. "And now, you're springing this engagement on them. We can't just forget the reasons that brought y'all back to Brooklyn in the first place." He paused, letting out a heavy sigh that filled the room with tension. "Every day, I find myself questioning your parenting choices, Nora."

Sensing the escalating tension, Sarah reached out and gently placed her hand on Mylan's shoulder, silently pleading with him to calm down.

Nora's face hardened, her eyebrows knitting together. "Excuse me, Mr. 'I've been a father for six months and now think I'm an expert on raising kids.'" Her voice was steady, but her clenched jaw and narrowed eyes displayed her frustration. "This was supposed to be a happy moment, and you're ruining it."

The tension in the room was obvious; Nora's posture was rigid, while the others at the table shifted uncomfortably, sensing the shift in mood from celebration to confrontation.

Mylan stood up swiftly, his frustration boiling over. "You barely know this man. And now, he's sitting here at family dinners with us before you've even sorted things out with your kids." He gestured dismissively towards Nora. "You're on some bullshit, and deep down, you know it."

Just then, the baby crying from another room cut through the heated exchange, giving the argument a short pause. Seizing the opportunity to escape the tension, Sage and Avery quickly volunteered to check on the baby. Once they left, the room's atmosphere shifted, heavy with unspoken words and unresolved issues.

Luke, sensing the strain his presence had caused, spoke up quietly. "I don't want to cause any issues between you two, so I think it would be best to leave. My apologies," he said, his tone sincere.

Nora's reaction was swift as she reached out, her hand clamped around Luke's forearm. "No, if he leaves, me and my children are leaving too." Her gaze was fierce, a silent challenge as she stared down Mylan.

Mylan's patience snapped. "Good. At least then I'll know mine, and I are safe without you around. Get your ass out of my place. Now!" His voice boomed across the room, leaving no room for argument.

Sarah intervened, her voice laced with concern. "Baby, you don't mean that," she said, her eyes locked with Mylan's in a plea for reason.

"Like hell I don't," Mylan shot back, his face twisted angrily.

Nora called Sage and Avery out, urging them to come on. Together, they gathered their things and left the condo, the tension in the room dissipating as the door closed behind them.

Sarah could see the turmoil etched into Mylan's posture; the rigidity of his shoulders spoke volumes. She gathered her dirty blonde hair, twisting it into a quick, messy bun atop her head before moving closer to him. Wrapping her arms around Mylan in a comforting embrace, she leaned in, her voice soft and reassuring. "Everything is going to be okay," she whispered, her breath warm against his ear.

Chapter 5

Collision

D r. McCoy's office was quiet and welcoming, away from the busy streets outside. The room had soft lighting and earthy colors that made it feel cozy. Nora and Avery sat on a big sofa across from Dr. McCoy, who was in his chair, ready to listen.

"How is everything going?" Dr. McCoy asked, her gaze shifted from Avery to Nora.

Avery remained silent, casting a brief glance at her mother before she crossed her arms defensively. Dr. McCoy, observing the unspoken dynamics at play, gently prodded, "I am sensing some tension between you two. Who would like to go first?" Her tone was neutral.

Just as Nora was about to speak, Avery quickly interjected. "She's getting married to a man who's ten years younger than her. They've only been together for about six months. She didn't even ask me or Sage how we felt about it before making such a big decision." Avery paused, taking a deep breath to gather her thoughts and emotions.

Dr. McCoy settled deeper into her seat, turning his attention to Nora, signaling it was her turn to respond.

"I don't need permission from my children on whom I can marry. And last I checked, you liked Luke. So, what's the problem?" Nora countered.

Seeing the need to pause and reflect on the exchange, Dr. McCoy gently interrupted. "Avery, it seems you have strong feelings about your mother's decision to get married. Why don't you share those feelings directly with Nora?"

Avery's words were laced with hurt, and her voice dropped slightly, "It doesn't matter what I say. She doesn't care how I feel. Just like when my dad died."

Nora's reaction was immediate; her gaze sharpened, sending a clear warning to Avery to tread lightly when discussing her father's death and the deeper, darker family secrets they harbored. These therapy sessions were supposed to be a step towards mending their fractured relationship, yet the problems of their past, especially Nora's involvement in her husband's demise, loomed large between them.

On the surface, it seemed their main issue was communication, but Avery felt the real problem ran deeper, rooted in the shadows of Nora's criminal past. This unspoken truth made their attempt to reconcile even more challenging.

"Tell her how you feel, Avery," Dr. McCoy encouraged gently, prompting a more open dialogue.

Turning towards her mother, Avery confessed, "Sometimes I feel like you would be better off without me."

Avery's admission struck Nora profoundly. She felt as if her heart had stopped, the words cutting through her with an intensity that left her momentarily breathless.

Avery's words flowed more freely now, each one heavy with emotion. "Every decision you've made since Dad died has only been for your benefit. You've never once asked me how I feel. It's always about Sage; you never see me. You never chose me." As she spoke, a single tear escaped, tracing a path down to her lips. "Why don't you ever choose me?" she implored, her voice breaking. Avery paused, "Why don't you love me?"

Nora felt overwhelmed, tears suddenly flooding her eyes. She stood abruptly, moving towards the wide window that offered a sprawling view of Manhattan below. For a moment, she tried to find her words, but they were caught in her throat, choked by the surge of feelings Avery's words had unleashed. Turning back to Avery, Nora could see the pain in her daughter's eyes. Slowly, she walked back from the window and sat down on the sofa again, closer to Avery this time.

Once again, Nora tried to speak, but words failed her at first. She wiped away her tears with the palm of her hand, gathering her thoughts. After a brief pause, she finally found her voice. "When I was your age, Avery... my relationship with my mother was strained. She treated me like I was unwanted, the odd one out. She told me that my father raped her, and when she looked at me, she saw him."

Nora paused, unconsciously biting her nail, a sign of her inner turmoil. "I swore that if I had children, I would never treat them the way she treated me. Yet here I am, realizing I've been treating you worse than she ever did me." The admission hung heavy in the room, a raw acknowledgment of her failures as a parent.

"Avery, I am truly sorry," Nora continued, her voice steady but filled with regret. "I know saying sorry doesn't change the fact that I haven't been there for you the way I should have. But I want to be better for you. I promise I will be better." Her words were a pledge, a vow to mend the rift between them and rebuild their relationship.

The session carried on for another 20 minutes, during which Dr. McCoy guided Nora and Avery through their emotions and thoughts, aiming to pave the way for healing. As they prepared to leave, Dr. McCoy gave them a homework assignment aimed at further mending their relationship. "I want you two to spend a day together next week, just the two of you, alone," she instructed. Avery and Nora nodded in agreement, ready to take this next step toward reconciliation.

***

The sound of the basketball hitting the gym floor echoed around them, a constant reminder of Cylus's growing frustration. Despite his best efforts, each shot he took stubbornly missed its mark. With every failed attempt, a growl of annoyance escaped him.

Sage entered the gym and immediately noticed his upset demeanor. "Hey babe," she said softly, hoping to offer some comfort.

He gave her a brief nod, his concentration briefly broken, but he didn't speak. Gathering his resolve, Cylus aimed for another shot. Yet, the ball bounced off the rim once more, adding to the series of misses that punctuated the silence of the gym.

Sage let her book bag fall to the floor as she dashed to retrieve the errant ball, tossing it back to him with an encouraging, "You got this."

Yet, his next attempt missed as well. Sage caught the rebound and approached him. "What's up? Why are you all in your head? Just focus on the net," she advised, trying to break through his frustration.

Cylus responded with defeat, snatching the ball away. "What do you think I'm doing?" he retorted, his narrowed eyes betraying his inner turmoil as he retreated to the bleachers.

Sage, not deterred, followed and sat beside him, her concern growing. She gently placed her hand on his shoulder. "Did I do something wrong?" she asked, her voice soft with worry.

He shifted away from her touch, standing up as if to put more distance between them. "Coach benched me for the season," he muttered, his voice barely above a whisper. A moment later, he hurled the ball across the gym in a gesture of resignation. "The doctor didn't clear me to play."

The revelation hung heavy in the air, explaining the source of his frustration but leaving a new tension between them.

Sage wrapped her arms around him in a comforting embrace. "I'm so sorry, but maybe this isn't such a bad thing. It gives you time to heal fully," she offered, trying to find a silver lining in his situation.

Cylus, however, was quick to pull away from her comfort. "You don't understand. This is my senior year," he said, frustration lacing his words. "There'll be colleges at every game. If I'm not on that court, there goes any chance of a scholarship."

Sage responded with a roll of her eyes, her attempt to inject some realism into the conversation. "Cylus, let's be real—your family is wealthy. They can get you into any university you want, and by then, I'm sure you'll be cleared to play."

Her words, meant to reassure, instead underscored the divide in their perspectives, highlighting the gap between his dreams and her practicality.

His frustration erupted, and he kicked the bench. "I want to earn my place in college on my own. I don't want to ask my parents for anything, and you know that" he snapped, taking a deep breath to calm himself. "You know what, just leave me alone."

"Why are you acting like this is all my fault?" Sage asked, her voice rising in confusion.

"Because it is!" he screamed back at her; the intensity in his voice caused Sage to step back, startled by the sudden outburst instinctively.

"If I hadn't met you, I wouldn't have gotten shot by your crazy ass aunt. Your whole family is messed up, and I don't want any part of that drama again. So, I'm done. I've got my own problems to deal with." With those harsh words, Cylus gathered his things in a swift motion and brushed past Sage, making his way toward the gym exit.

Sage felt her eyes well up at his words, the sting of his rejection sharp and sudden. But she fought back the tears, refusing to let them fall. She took a deep breath, steadying herself against the wave of emotions that threatened to overwhelm her.

Tegan caught up to Sage outside the school, her sudden appearance startling Sage out of her thoughts. Immediately noticing the redness in Sage's eyes, Tegan's expression shifted to one of concern. "What happened?" she questioned, her voice filled with worry.

Taking a deep breath, Sage lifted her gaze, coincidentally catching sight of Cylus laughing and exiting the school surrounded by cheerleaders. The sight twisted something inside her, making the situation feel all the more real.

Following Sage's gaze, Tegan spotted Cylus and pieced the situation together quickly. "Did you and Cylus break up?" she proceeded cautiously.

With a heavy heart, Sage simply nodded, confirming Tegan's suspicions without a word.

Without another word, Tegan wrapped Sage in a comforting embrace. "Boys suck," she declared.

Sage managed a slight smile in response, finding a brief moment of laughter in their shared sentiment. "They sure do," she agreed.

Their moment was briefly interrupted by the sound of a car horn. Tegan glanced over to see it was her brother signaling her, and she gave Sage one more reassuring hug. "You going to be okay? Want my brother to drop you home?" she offered, her concern evident.

Sage shook her head gently. "No, I'm good. I'm about to meet up with Avery. I'll see you tomorrow," she said, her voice steady, signaling a strength she was starting to gather within herself.

As Sage and Cylus's paths crossed outside the school, their eyes met for a fleeting moment before he turned away, heading across the street with his friends. Sage's gaze lingered on him for a second longer.

From a distance, Sage spotted Avery approaching, her presence a welcome sight amid the day's turmoil. Eager to leave the tension behind and cross the street to meet her sister, Sage stepped off the curb.

In an instant, a car, coming seemingly out of nowhere, struck Sage. The impact sent a shockwave of panic through everyone nearby. Avery and Cylus, witnessing the horrifying scene unfold, sprinted towards her, along with several other bystanders.

Chapter 6

Crossroads

Nora rushed to the receptionist at the hospital's front desk, her heart pounding. Before she could ask a question, Avery screamed out to her. The concern on Avery's face was unmistakable, and Cylus stood next to her, looking equally worried.

Tegan came running in, breathless from the call she'd gotten from Cylus. Luke was right behind her, his face tense.

"What the hell happened?" Nora demanded.

"I don't know. She stepped out on the street to come to me, and a car just came out of nowhere. Almost like it was waiting for her," Avery explained frantically. She jumped up when she saw Mylan come rushing in.

Nora and Mylan hadn't spoken since she stormed out of his place a few days ago. Mylan embraced Avery with a tight hug. "What happened?" he asked.

Cylus stood up, his face grim. "Sage was hit by a car."

Mylan questioned Avery and Cylus about the car's make and model. Cylus explained that he saw an Escalade.

"Was it black?" Luke asked.

Everyone focused their eyes on Luke as Cylus nodded. Mylan walked closer to him, backing him into a wall. "Who was it?"

Luke asked about the license plate number, and Cylus remembered that it started with a V. Luke shook his head.

"Is it who I think it is?" Nora asked, her eyes fixed on Luke. "She better hope nothing is wrong with my daughter, or I swear—"

Nora was cut off by a familiar voice. "This is starting to feel like déjà vu," Detective Douglas said, with Detective Matthew right beside him.

Nora let out a deep sigh. Just then, the doctor informed Nora that she could see Sage now, but only two people were allowed. Nora and Avery headed toward her room.

Avery rushed to Sage's bedside and gave her a tight hug. "Are you okay?"

Sage smiled. "I'm actually fine. I only sprained my ankle. They're giving me crutches. I only need to be on them for two weeks."

Detective Douglas and Matthew wasted no time. "Hi Sage, it's unfortunate that we have to meet again under such circumstances. Would you be okay with us asking a few questions?"

Sage glanced at Nora to get the okay to speak with them. Nora nodded, giving her permission. Sage agreed to be questioned.

"What happened?" Matthew asked.

Sage and Avery explained everything down to the black Escalade and the license plate, starting with the letter V. Douglas asked to speak with Nora alone, and Matthew stayed with the girls.

"Is there anything that I should know?" Douglas asked.

Nora looked through the glass at the girls, debating whether to keep Veronica's identity private and handle it herself or leave it to the police. With a heavy heart, she chose to let the police handle it this time. "Her name is Veronica Segan. Wife of the late Harry Segan. He used to own Onyx."

Douglas let out a soft chuckle. "The casino that your boyfriend now owns. I think I might have an idea why she would want to come after you and your family."

"Listen to me; if she comes after my family again, I am going to kill her. Do you understand me?" Nora said, her voice cold and steady.

Douglas sighed. "I'm going to act like I didn't hear that. I'll get my team on it and keep in touch." He knocked on the glass, signaling for Matthew to come. "Nora, don't do anything stupid."

Nora crossed her arms and watched Douglas and Matthew disappear down the hall. Just as she was about to enter Sage's room, she heard a commotion coming from the waiting area. She rushed over to see Mylan and Luke arguing.

Nora stepped in the middle of them. "What the hell is going on?"

"You brought this man into our life, and now Sage is sitting in the hospital," Mylan yelled.

Nora looked over at a frightened Cylus and Tegan. She gestured for them to leave, assuring them that Sage would call later. She watched until they disappeared down the hall.

"You two need to cut this shit out," she said, turning back to Mylan and Luke. "And as for you," she gestured to Mylan, "What happened to Sage is not Luke's fault. That bitch Veronica is coming for what she thinks belongs to her."

"Because it does," Mylan's voice grew louder. "You two idiots took over her husband's casino and left her with nothing. I would be coming after y'all, too." Mylan glared at Luke. "I don't trust you. I know you used my sister to take down Harry so you could get control over the casino."

Nora looked around, anxious about who might be listening. "Keep your voice down," she hissed.

A nurse walked in and asked them to leave. Before Mylan exited the waiting room, he turned to face Luke. "If anything else happens to my family, consider this a warning: prepare for your funeral."

Later, Nora sat in a corner, watching Sage and Avery play hand games in the hospital room. She nervously bit down on her French manicure, staring out the window. Thoughts of Veronica making another move on her family were driving her crazy. Her worry was momentarily interrupted when she looked up to see Paulette in the doorway.

"I hope I'm not interrupting. Hey, Baby," Paulette greeted Sage warmly as she handed her a card.

Nora greeted her, and Sage explained that she had invited Paulette. Sage thanked her for the card.

"It's from Warren." Paulette paused, her expression softening. "He wanted to be here, but he wasn't sure."

Nora thanked Paulette for coming to visit. Meanwhile, Avery stepped out to go to the vending machine. With a concerned look, Paulette glanced between Nora and Sage. "Was this an accident or on purpose?"

Nora and Sage exchanged looks. Nora reassured her, "You have nothing to worry about, Ms. Paulette. It's being handled by the police." She gently rubbed Sage's leg under the sheet, adding, "Everything will be okay."

"Anything involving my granddaughter is something for me to worry about. If there is something or someone coming after y'all, it is important that Warren and I know about it so we can handle it as a family," Paulette assured firmly. "There will be no investigation if there's not a body to find." She winked at Nora, and a slight smile grew on her face.

Nora caught the implication behind Paulette's words, her mind racing with the gravity of the suggestion. At that moment, the unspoken understanding hung heavily in the air: Veronica had to die. This realization deepened the already tense atmosphere, pushing Nora to confront the looming threat more directly, perhaps even outside the bounds of the law.

Chapter 7

Unveiling

The diner was empty, the air tinged with the comforting smell of freshly brewed coffee and the faint aroma of grilled sandwiches. The scent of baked goods from the morning rush lingered, blending with the subtle sharpness of cleaning products. Overhead, the gentle hum of a ceiling fan mixed with the low murmur of a classic rock tune playing softly through speakers, creating a relaxed, almost nostalgic atmosphere.

A waitress, her apron slightly stained from the day's work, walked over to the table with a welcoming smile. "Would you like to order a drink until the rest of your party comes?"

"Yeah, let me get a green tea, no sugar. Thank you," Nora responded, settling into the booth with a view of the entrance.

As the waitress stepped away, Warren walked up behind Nora and slid into the seat across from her. "You sure love your green tea, no sugar combo," he commented, his smile warm and familiar, breaking the quiet tension that seemed to linger around Nora.

The waitress returned shortly with Nora's green tea and took their orders efficiently. The service was swift, and their food arrived quickly, filling the table with the inviting aromas of a hearty diner meal. They began eating, the initial small talk fading into a more contemplative silence.

Nora looked up from her food, her movements slow as she wiped her mouth with a napkin. Her voice was soft and filled with concern, but as she mentioned the name, her eyes clouded with sadness. "I was just checking in to see how you have been since..." she trailed off, the weight of the memory pressing down. "Donny."

Warren's reaction was almost immediate. His body tensed visibly, a discomfort that crept into his posture. He shifted in his seat, his shoulders tightening, and his gaze dropped briefly to the table before meeting Nora's eyes again. His hands, which had been relaxed moments before, now were clasped tightly together, knuckles whitening.

"I've had better days, but I don't want to talk about that," he said quickly. He paused, taking a deep breath as if bracing himself for what he needed to ask next. "I want to talk about what happened to Sage, and please, Nora, tell me the truth."

Nora spilled everything, leaving no detail untouched as she recounted the first phone call from Veronica six months prior. As she spoke, Warren's expression hardened, his appetite fading as the gravity of the situation settled in. He pushed his plate away and clenched his jaw, a visible sign of his growing frustration and resolve.

"What's the plan?" he asked, sitting up straighter in his seat, his eyes locked onto Nora.

"The police are going to handle this one," Nora replied firmly. "I don't want to be involved in another shoot-out. It's not worth it, and you, of all people should know that."

Warren's response was skeptical, and his brows furrowed as he leaned forward, placing both elbows on the table, his hands clasped tightly. "I never thought I'd see the day when you'd back down from a threat," he said, his voice low but intense. "You need to put her down because if you don't, she is going to come after not only Sage but Avery, too."

His words hung in the air, a stark reminder of the stakes they were dealing with, urging Nora to reconsider the dangers of letting the law handle Veronica without any direct intervention from their side.

Nora acknowledged Warren's logic but was adamant about approaching the situation differently this time. She hesitated, the weight of past actions heavy on her shoulders.

"Donny died because of us. I don't want any more blood on my hands," she confessed, her voice thick with regret.

"He died because we didn't know who the threat was, and now we do. We have to get her before she comes for us," Warren countered, his resolve firm. His insistence reflected his determination to prevent history from repeating itself.

Nora shook her head, her frustration evident. "She already came for us, and what's all this talk about 'us'? This is my problem."

Warren leaned forward, his expression intense. "Sage may hate me for the rest of her life, but I'll do anything to protect her. If that means going toe to toe with this bitch, then so be it."

Their intense exchange was suddenly interrupted by a familiar voice. "Am I interrupting something?" The tone was light, but the timing could have been more convenient.

Nora looked up to see Luke standing at the entrance of the diner. She offered a tired smile and asked, "What are you doing here?"

Luke explained as he approached their booth, "I was just driving past and saw your car." He greeted Warren with a friendly dap, the casual exchange contrasting with the tension at the table.

Warren, sensing it was time to leave, stood up from the booth. "I'm just heading out," he told Nora, his tone serious.

"Remember what we talked about." He laid some money on the table to cover the bill and quickly made his way out, leaving a palpable silence behind.

Luke slid into the booth where Warren had been sitting. "What was that about?" he asked, his eyes searching Nora's face for clues.

Nora sighed, feeling the weight of the conversation she'd just had. "We were talking about Sage and what to do about Veronica, but I decided to leave it to the detectives to handle it."

Luke's expression hardened. "Why would you do that? Do you think they will save you if something happens? Because they won't. You saw what happened to that Donny kid. I'm trying to protect you and the girls. You need to tell the detectives to stop the investigation."

His words echoed Warren's urgency but with a hint of desperation that suggested his personal stakes in the matter were high, complicating Nora's already difficult situation.

"That's not how that works. Whether or not I want them to stop the investigation, they're still going to do their job. What does it matter anyway?" Nora countered, her voice tinged with skepticism.

Luke leaned forward, his expression earnest. "Listen, there's a charity gala that Veronica hosts every year for education for underprivileged children. It's coming up soon," he explained, his voice lowering. "It's a big event, lots of influential people attend. It could be the perfect opportunity for you to talk to her face to face."

Nora furrowed her brows, the idea immediately setting off alarms in her mind. "That doesn't sound like a good idea," she expressed her concerns, shaking her head slightly. "Confronting Veronica in such a public and possibly heavily guarded event could backfire. It sounds risky, and it might just escalate things even further."

"Listen, the best way to end this is by talking to her. What's the worst that can happen?" Luke asked, his tone suggesting that a direct approach might simplify their complications.

Nora shot back, her voice laced with realism, "We can be killed by her goons, and no one would say a word about it. They'll just find our bodies floating around somewhere at Coney Island. That's what can happen. We don't have a team, no backup. We would be two fishes in a sea full of sharks."

Luke, noticing her anxiety, tried another angle. "We can get Warren to come with us for backup. I'm sure he'd do anything for you," he said, his eyes narrowed, trying to reassure her with the mention of Warren's support, hoping to boost her confidence in the plan.

Her brow furrowed deeply, and her eyes flickered with the shadows of doubt. Each thought seemed to carve a deeper line of worry across her features, reflecting her internal struggle between retaliation and caution.

"Baby, she tried to kill Sage. End her!" Luke's words were meant to stoke a fire of resolve, but they also summoned the haunting echo of Detective Douglas's stern warning: Nora, don't do anything stupid.

Nora's expression shifted as she wrestled with the conflict between vengeance and wisdom. The doubt that clouded her gaze began to clear, replaced by a steely glint of determination. Revenge burned within her, a dangerous spark that threatened to consume her usual judgment.

She looked up at Luke, her eyes now sharp, "Give me the details on the Gala," she demanded, her voice steady, almost cold.

Chapter 8

The Gala

The gala was a lavish affair, set on the sprawling grounds of Veronica's Long Island mansion, which was adorned with meticulous care. The estate itself was a marvel of luxury, with manicured gardens illuminated by gentle fairy lights that twinkled like stars scattered across the grounds.

Inside, the mansion buzzed with the chatter of the wealthy attendees. Men in sharp, perfectly tailored suits mingled with women in dazzling evening gowns, their laughter and the clink of fine crystal filling the air. A live orchestra played soft classical music, adding a layer of sophisticated ambiance to the evening.

Nora, Luke, and Warren arrived, dressed impeccably. Nora was stunning in an elegant black dress that was both sophisticated and commanding. Luke and Warren matched her in style, both in sleek, dark suits and ties, their attire speaking of careful preparation and a determination to blend in yet stand out.

As they moved through the crowd, Warren leaned in, his voice low with concern, "I don't know about this. We should be meeting her on our terms."

Before Nora could respond, Luke, who had been scanning the room, interrupted. "There she is," he whispered, nodding subtly toward a figure across the room.

Veronica stood surrounded by a group of admirers, laughing gracefully at something said. She was the picture of charm and poise, dressed in an exquisite gown that likely cost more than most people made in a year, her demeanor that of a hostess in complete control of her domain.

As they watched her, the trio felt the weight of what they were about to undertake. This was not just a social event; it was a battlefield, and they were right in the heart of enemy territory.

Veronica Segan captured the stage with an aura that was both commanding and chilling, dressed in a maroon maxi dress that clung to her like a second skin. The off-the-shoulder cut added a touch of daring to her look, perfectly offset by her brown hair, which was swept up into a sleek updo secured with gold chopsticks that glinted under the stage lights.

As she reached the microphone, her gaze swept across the audience, locking onto Nora with a deliberate intensity. With a sly smile and a quick wink directed at Nora, Veronica began, her voice smooth but edged with a frosty undertone.

"Welcome to my humble abode. You all look amazing," she announced, her voice dripping with charm yet undercut by the coldness in her eyes. Those eyes, icy and calculating, seemed to drill into Nora, sending a clear message of challenge and warning.

Nora subtly signaled to Warren and Luke to position themselves strategically on opposite sides of the expansive room, ensuring a broad view in case of any unexpected events. While Veronica captivated the audience with her polished delivery, Nora remained vigilant, her hand occasionally brushing against the fabric of her dress where a gun was discreetly holstered around her thigh, hidden from the unknowing eyes of the gala attendees.

As Veronica's speech flowed seamlessly, Nora's attention was abruptly drawn away by a familiar face in the crowd. Celine Graves, a figure from her darker past, was whispering into the ear of a well-dressed man. Their eyes met, and a wave of confusion crossed Celine's face. With a subtle nod, Celine signaled Nora to follow her to a more secluded area.

Quietly excusing herself, Nora followed Celine into a dimly lit hallway, away from the prying eyes and ears of the gala. They faced each other, a momentary silence hung between them before they both began to speak simultaneously.

"What are you..." they both paused, realizing the irony.

"There is no way you're here donating to charity," Celine smirked, her voice low but edged with a playful accusation.

"And I guess that old man you were speaking to was your grandfather and not a customer," Nora retorted, matching Celine's tone, a hint of sarcasm lacing her words.

"Touché bitch. So tell me what you've been up to? Kill anybody lately." Her eyes sparkled with mischief and intrigue as she leaned against the wall, her posture relaxed yet clearly expecting a tale as complex as the life Nora led.

Luke swiftly appeared in the hallway, his expression urgent. "Veronica is almost done with her speech," he informed Nora, clearly ready to jump into whatever plan they had next.

Nora nodded, her gaze flicked back to Celine. "Go back to your post, Luke. We need to keep eyes on her," she instructed firmly, dismissing him with a wave of her hand.

As Luke turned to leave, Celine's grip tightened on Nora's forearm, her curiosity piqued. "Tell me what's going on. Who was that?"

Nora's face hardened, a shadow passing over her features. "It's best that you don't know. Wouldn't want your business to crumble messing with me," she replied.

Celine's eyes narrowed, and her voice dropped to a whisper. "If you're thinking about going up against Veronica Segan, you better think twice. She will destroy you and everything you love."

Nora's response was immediate. "Veronica already came for me, and now I'm going for blood. She started this, but I'm going to finish it."

Their intense conversation was abruptly cut off as two men approached. Celine stepped back, her eyes wide as she assessed the threat. Nora and Celine exchanged a quick, significant look, a silent acknowledgment of the danger Nora was walking into.

Without warning, the men grabbed Nora by her arms, their grip firm and unyielding as they escorted her further down the hallway. Celine watched helplessly, her heart racing until they disappeared around a corner. Left alone, she was torn between following them and staying out of harm's way; her mind raced with concern for Nora.

Nora was led into a room that seemed tailored for intimidation. Three men stood like statues in each corner, dressed entirely in black, their arms held rigidly behind their backs—a silent display of discipline and threat. As Nora was patted down, the cold hands of the guards confirmed her vulnerability as they took her gun from its holster, stripping her of her only weapon. The tension in the room spiked.

Then, Veronica entered her smile as sharp and cutting as a knife. She exuded a controlled aura of menace that filled the space between them.

They stood face to face, Veronica's smile never wavering. "To what do I owe the pleasure?" she asked, her voice smooth but laced with an edge that hinted at the danger beneath.

Nora, despite being outnumbered and now unarmed, maintained her composure. "What do you want?" she asked, direct and undeterred.

"That's such a vague question. I thought, as a former detective, you would come better than that." Veronica began to circle Nora slowly, her gaze appraising. "But since you asked. I want my husband and son back. Obviously, that can't happen, so I'll take the casino instead."

The starkness of Veronica's demand hung heavily in the air, framing the depths of her vendetta and the lengths she was willing to go to reclaim what she perceived as hers. Veronica's movements around Nora were predatory, emphasizing that this was her domain and Nora was merely a player in her game.

Nora's proposal was a desperate gambit, an attempt to defuse the situation and perhaps find an unlikely ally in

Veronica. "What if we were partners instead? Own the casino together," she suggested, her voice steady despite the tension.

Veronica paused, stepping back as she contemplated the offer. Her expression was unreadable for a moment before her features settled into a frown. "In order for us to work together, I would have to like you, and I don't. You, your little mutt daughter, psychotic sister, and that ungrateful bastard nephew of mine stole from me. So working together is not an option."

Nora bit back her response, choosing silence over escalating the confrontation.

"I have to give it to you, though. You are bold, bringing your raggedy ass here. Did you think I wouldn't notice that humongous forehead of yours?" Veronica's tone was mocking, her words designed to provoke.

"That's enough," Nora finally snapped, her voice rising in defiance against Veronica's taunts.

"No, it's enough when I say it's enough," Veronica yelled back, her voice echoing off the walls of the room. "You came into my event without an invitation. I will say and do whatever the hell I want."

The room tensed further, the air thick with animosity as both women stood their ground, a clash not just of words but of wills, setting the stage for a confrontation that seemed inevitable.

"What happens if I don't turn over the casino?" Nora asked, her gaze intense, locked firmly on Veronica's eyes, betraying no fear.

They held each other's stare, and though it lasted only a second, the moment stretched out, heavy with the weight of unspoken threats. Veronica's expression shifted; her lips curled into a small, sinister smile as she reached out to gently caress Nora's cheek with her soft but dangerously sharp-nailed hands. "You will be attending a funeral every single week," she whispered chillingly close, her voice soft but filled with deadly promise.

Her nail traced delicately down Nora's cheek to her neck, where she made a small 'X' with the tip. "I will be generous. You have two weeks to sign over the papers," Veronica stated, her tone casual as if discussing something as mundane as the weather, yet the threat behind her words was palpable and terrifying.

Veronica was not a woman to be underestimated. Nora, realizing the gravity of the situation, knew she was in a dangerous position, one that would require all her wits and resources to navigate safely.

Nora stumbled backward, bumping into one of the men positioned like statues around the room. Veronica's eyes never left Nora as she sharply snapped her fingers, causing all her men to stand at attention instantly.

"Get this bitch out of my place," Veronica commanded, her gaze pierced through Nora with disdain.

Nora felt a firm hand clamp around her arm, the grip iron-tight and unyielding. She struggled, trying to pull away, but the man's strength was overwhelming. As she was being forcibly led away, Veronica called out one last taunt.

"Next time you bring backup, make sure they back you up," she said, her words cutting deep, emphasizing her control over the situation and mocking Nora's failed attempt at intimidation.

As Nora was forcefully dragged away, her brow furrowed deeply, eyes darted from Veronica to the men escorting her. Her confusion manifested as a slight shake of the head, a brief squint as if to focus better, and a tightening of her lips. "What the hell is that supposed to mean?" she yelled, her voice echoed down the hallway as she attempted to wrench her arm free from the steely grip of her escort.

Veronica's laughter followed her, a sound that seemed to bounce off the grand walls, mocking her. Nora's shouts grew louder as she was propelled towards the exit.

As Nora stumbled out of the mansion, disoriented and fuming, she was met by Celine, who had been watching the entire scene unfold. Celine ran out after her, her eyes wide with concern. "You want to tell me what the hell is going on now?" she demanded.

Luke was thrown out next, landing heavily beside them. Nora immediately gripped his hand, and a look of panic flashed across her face. "Where is Warren?" she asked, her voice strained.

Luke shook his head. "I don't know. I thought he was thrown out, too," he replied, glancing around as if hoping Warren would appear.

The three of them stood together, staring up at the imposing mansion. The glory of the building now seemed sinister, each window and shadow a possible sign of the danger inside.

"If Warren is still in there, he's not coming back out," Luke said grimly. "Everything she does is not by accident. She's calculated, and every move she makes is for a reason."

Nora clenched her jaw, her eyes narrowed as she considered Luke's words. She knew he was right.

"What did you get yourself into, Nora? Veronica Segan is not your typical opp. That woman will kill you and everyone close to you," Celine warned.

Nora narrowed her eyes at Celine, suspicion creeping in. "Then why are you still here?"

Celine crossed her arms, her gaze steady. "Because you got Warren involved once again, and if you plan to go up against her, you're going to need an army. Lucky for you, I'm not still holding a grudge."

Nora's eyes remained fixed on the imposing mansion; her mind raced with thoughts of revenge. Her face hardened, a fierce determination taking over. "I'm going to burn this muthafucker down," she muttered, her voice low but firm.

Luke and Celine exchanged a glance, recognizing the seriousness of Nora's intent. This was no idle threat; Nora was ready to go to war, and they would need to be prepared for the fallout.

Chapter 9

Ultimatum

Nora, Sage, and Avery were sitting in the kitchen, the quiet hum of the refrigerator the only sound filling the room. Suddenly, a hard, insistent knock echoed through the apartment, startling them. The forceful sound was sharp, like a hammer striking metal.

Nora stood up, her heart pounding, and walked cautiously to the door. She peered through the peephole and took a deep breath before unlocking it. As she opened the door, Detective Douglas pushed his way inside without waiting for an invitation.

"Where is he?" he demanded, his voice sharp and urgent.

"First of all, don't just walk into my apartment like that. And where is who?" Nora shot back, her irritation clear.

Detective Douglas began pacing back and forth like a caged animal desperate to escape, his energy barely contained. "Don't play stupid. Warren Layfette? Where is

Warren?" His eyes bore into her, filled with frustration and desperation.

"How am I supposed to know?" Nora said, her voice steady but laced with frustration.

"You were the last person he was with, according to Paulette. Four nights ago, he went with you and Luke to Long Island. Don't deny it," Douglas pressed, his gaze unwavering.

Sage stood up from the table, her eyes wide with worry. "Where is he, Mom?"

Nora looked at everyone, the weight of the situation pressing heavily on her shoulders. She sighed deeply, her voice barely above a whisper. "Veronica has him."

"Damn it," Douglas exclaimed, slamming his fist against the wall in a rare display of anger. "I told you to let me handle her." His frustration was obvious.

"She hit my daughter with a damn car. I don't have time to wait for you to do your little investigation. She is coming after my whole family if Luke and I don't sign over the casino to her," Nora snapped, her voice shaking with anger.

"Then give her the stupid casino, Mom," Avery interjected, her voice trembling. "It's not worth one of us really getting hurt or killed."

Nora looked at both Sage and Avery, her heart aching at the fear in their eyes. She began to pace back and forth, her mind racing with the weight of the decision. "I want to give it to her, but Luke says she is going to kill us anyway," she said.

Douglas stood with both hands on his hips. "What reason would she have to harm anyone if you give her back what she wants?" he asked his tone more measured.

Nora, Sage, and Avery exchanged looks, a silent communication passing between them before they turned their attention back to Detective Douglas. He noticed the exchange and tilted his head, suspicion etched across his features. "That is the only reason she is coming after you, right? Because if there is something else I need to know..."

"There's nothing else," Sage quickly responded, her voice firm.

Avery, however, interjected with a different concern. "Uncle Mylan doesn't trust Luke. He thinks Luke is up to something, and I agree." She narrowed her eyes at Nora, the doubt clear in her gaze. "Something's not right with him."

Nora brushed off Avery's comment, choosing to focus on the immediate threat. "I will speak with Luke, and we will sign the papers over. The last thing I want is to put my family in danger again." Her voice was resolute, but the uncertainty in her eyes hinted at the complex layers of distrust and fear that had always been part of their lives.

Later that night, Sage and Avery went to Mylan's condo to give Nora and Luke some privacy. Luke sat at the dinner table across from Nora as they ate. Nora was barely touching her food, her fork idly pushing pieces around her plate. She looked up at Luke and stared at him until he noticed.

"You look like you have something on your mind," he said, putting his fork down and leaning slightly forward.

"I think we should give the casino back to Veronica," Nora said, her voice steady but strained. "At this point, it does not make any sense to keep fighting. Sage got hit by a car, and now she has Warren. I can't let this go any further."

Luke's expression hardened, and he leaned back, crossing his arms. "You really think giving her what she wants will make her stop? She'll see it as weakness and come after us even harder."

Nora shook her head, frustration etched in her features. "And if we keep the casino, what then? More of our family gets hurt, or worse? I can't take that risk. We need to end this, and if that means giving her the casino, then so be it."

Luke stared at her, his jaw clenched. "You don't understand. Veronica's not just after the casino. She wants control, and she'll take us out one by one to get it. Giving her the casino won't change that."

"Then what's your plan, Luke? Because right now, I don't see any other way to keep my family safe." Nora said.

Luke pushed his food away from him and wiped his mouth with a napkin. "Listen, I understand your concern, but I still have connections to some of her men. All we have to do is get a little aggressive to scare her off. That's it."

"And what about Warren? She will kill him if we do anything," Nora countered, her voice shaking with worry.

"She needs him for leverage. She isn't going to hurt him. Trust me," he assured her, pulling his plate back towards him and resuming his meal.

Nora looked at him, suspicion flickering in her eyes. She took a sip of her drink, buying herself a moment to think. "Why should I trust you?"

Luke slowly looked up from his food, a sinister glint in his eyes. "What the hell do you mean, why? I killed my uncle for you."

"Did you?" Nora challenged, her voice cold. "The main person to benefit from his death was you. It's just funny how you had no idea that if he died, the casino would be yours." She studied his face intently, searching for any sign of deceit.

"Is this about your brother not trusting me? Nora, I have done nothing to make you think bad of me. I didn't know that the casino would be given to me. Killing my uncle was never my plan, but I did it to protect you and your family because I love you," Luke said, his eyes sincere and pleading.

Nora searched his face for any sign of deceit, but his expression was earnest. She had no proof that he was lying, and the weight of his words and the emotion in his eyes convinced her. "I'm sorry. I just have a lot on my mind, and I second-guess myself. I know I can trust you, but I can't trust your judgment on this Veronica situation. I just think if we sign the papers, she will leave us alone."

"If that's what you want to do, then fine, but if we do this, you must know that she is not going to stop. Her son and husband are dead. Getting the casino back is just part of her plan," Luke warned, his voice heavy with concern.

"Well, I'd rather take that chance. And weren't you the one who said to talk face to face so we could end it? Why are you switching up now?" Nora shot back, frustration creeping into her tone.

"Because she took Warren. That's not the action of someone who wants to kiss and make up," Luke replied, his voice rising.

"I said what I said. We are signing those damn papers and moving on with our lives," Nora insisted, her voice firm and unwavering.

Luke stared at her, clearly conflicted but sensing her determination. "Alright, if that's what you want. But just know, we need to be prepared for whatever she throws at us next."

***

Nora sat in her office at the casino, the weight of recent events pressing heavily on her. The room was dimly lit, casting long shadows across her desk as she pored over the documents. The sound of a knock at the door startled her, and she looked up, her face going blank as she watched Paulette walk in and shut the door behind her.

Nora stood up and came around her desk to greet her, but the tension in Paulette's posture stopped her in her tracks. Paulette's expression was rigid, her eyes filled with a mix of fear and anger.

"Where is my son?" Paulette demanded, her tone sharp and unyielding.

Nora swallowed hard, trying to find her voice, but no words came out. She looked down at the floor, her eyes tracing the intricate shapes in the carpet, searching for some kind of grounding in the swirling storm of her thoughts. The silence stretched out painfully, thick with unspoken words.

Paulette, unable to contain her frustration, slammed her pocketbook onto the table; the sound echoed in the quiet room. "Don't you dare look away from me, Nora. Where is Warren?" she demanded, her eyes boring into Nora's, demanding an answer.

"The police are doing everything to find him," Nora explained, her voice trembling. She felt herself shrinking, almost regressing to a childlike state under Paulette's intense gaze, much like when her mother used to yell at her.

Paulette's face hardened as she opened her brown pocketbook and pulled out a small concealed gun, placing it deliberately on the desk. The threat was clear, and the gesture meant to intimidate. "I do not want to hear anything about what the police are doing," she said, her voice cold.

Nora took a deep breath, steadying herself. "Paulette, if I were you, I would put that away because we both know you don't know how to use it."

Paulette's eyes flashed with anger. Nora held her gaze, trying to project confidence despite the fear gnawing at her insides.

"That's Ms. Paulette to you," she snapped, her voice dripping with venom. "You think you're so tough, but we both know you're just a scary bitch. I have given you chance after chance, and now your chances have run out. So either you tell me what happened to Warren, or you and this entire casino will be up in flames."

Nora hesitated, her mind racing. She took a deep breath, trying to steady her nerves. "Like I said, the police are handling it. Now I am going to have to ask you to please leave these premises."

Paulette chuckled darkly as she picked up her gun, her eyes scanning the office with a manic gleam. With a swift motion, she slid the barrel back and began firing wildly, the deafening sound of gunshots reverberating through the room. Papers flew, glass shattered, and Nora ducked for cover as her heart raced.

"Where is Warren?" Paulette screamed, her voice cracked with desperation. Every time she spoke, the gun went off, emphasizing her words with deadly intent.

The racket of gunshots echoed throughout the casino, causing guests to scream and scatter, seeking cover from the unexpected violence. Chaos erupted as the once-calm atmosphere transformed into a scene of panic and fear.

"What the hell is wrong with you?" Nora screamed. She crawled over to her desk drawer, her hands shaking as she pulled out her pistol. She pointed it at Paulette, her eyes narrowing with resolve. "Put the damn gun down, now."

Paulette and Nora stood face to face, both women breathing heavily, their eyes locked in an intense stare. Despite Paulette's age, there was a fierce determination in her gaze, a fearlessness that came from years of hardship and survival. She did not back down, her grip on the gun unwavering.

Nora did not want to harm Paulette. This woman had been like a second mother to her growing up. With a deep breath, Nora slowly lowered her gun. "Veronica Segan," she finally said, her voice steady.

Paulette's eyes narrowed as she lowered her gun slightly. "Where can I find her?" she demanded, her voice still thick with anger and desperation.

Nora shook her head. "I can't send you into the lion's den, Paulette. It's too dangerous."

Before Paulette could respond, the office door burst open, and Detective Douglas and Matthew stormed in, guns drawn and ready. The tension in the room spiked as the two detectives took in the chaotic scene.

"Drop your weapons!" Douglas shouted, his eyes darting between Nora and Paulette.

Nora quickly jumped in front of Paulette, her hands raised in a placating gesture. "Don't shoot! Don't shoot! It's okay, just lower your guns," she pleaded, her voice urgent.

Paulette dropped the gun, and Matthew quickly moved in to cuff her, escorting her out of the office and down the hall. Once they disappeared, Douglas swiftly closed the door behind them.

"What the hell was that? You know what, I don't even want to know," he said, exasperation clear in his voice. He glanced at the door and then turned back to Nora, his expression serious. "My captain doesn't want me to go after

Veronica. Even after I told him about Sage being hit and now Warren missing."

"Why the hell not? We have enough evidence, at least for a search warrant, to look for the car that hit Sage," Nora replied, shaking her head in disbelief. "That doesn't make sense."

Douglas sighed, his frustration palpable. "There's also something going on with Matthew. When I brought up investigating Veronica, he completely brushed me off, and so did Captain Langford. I don't know, but I'm willing to bet she has them both on her payroll."

Nora walked behind her desk and placed her gun in the drawer, the metallic clink echoing the weight of her decision. She looked up at Douglas. "What am I supposed to do now? If the cops aren't willing to go after her, where does that leave my family and me?"

As Douglas and Nora stood in tense silence, a sudden knock on the door startled them both. A guard entered, carrying a small package. He handed it to Nora without a word, then exited the office, closing the door behind him. Nora examined the package, noting the absence of a return address. The only thing written on the box was a chilling message: "Tik Tok." Nora's heart skipped a beat as she turned the package over in her hands.

Nora looked at Douglas, a sense of dread washing over her. Using a paper cutter, she carefully sliced the box open. Her hand trembled a little as she reached inside and pulled out a ziplock bag. Inside was a severed finger, the blood still fresh and vivid. She dropped it back in the box, a lump forming in her throat as nausea threatened to overwhelm her. The dark complexion of the finger left no doubt in her mind; it was Warren's.

Chapter 10

Confrontation

Sage stood outside the imposing gray walls of the county jail; the building loomed over her. The air was thick with tension, and the distant sounds of the city buzzed around her. She took a deep breath, clutching the strap of her purse tightly as if it were a lifeline anchoring her to the moment.

After passing through the security checks, with the cold scrutiny of the guards making her heart race, Sage was led down a long, sterile hallway. The clang of the metal doors closing behind her sent a shiver down her spine, each one echoing like a reminder of where she was.

Finally, she stepped into the visiting room, a cold, impersonal space with rows of metal tables and chairs anchored to the floor. Kamari sat at one of the tables, her hair pulled back in a tight ponytail. Despite the orange jumpsuit and the harsh fluorescent lighting, she radiated a quiet strength that made her seem larger than life.

Sage approached, her stomach churning with nerves. She pulled out a chair and sat across from Kamari, her hands gripping the edge of the table. Their eyes met, and Sage could feel the unspoken tension in the air— a mix of warmth and defiance flickering in Kamari's gaze.

"I see your mother finally gave you my letters," Kamari said, her eyes sharp.

"You sent me a letter?" Sage's brow furrowed in confusion, her fingers nervously tapping the edge of the table. "She didn't give it to me, but I understand why." Her voice wavered, the weight of unspoken truths hanging heavily in the air between them.

Kamari's expression softened, though a flicker of frustration lingered in her eyes. "How'd you manage to get in here without a guardian?" she asked, leaning in a bit closer.

Sage hesitated before answering. "I used a fake ID. Tegan helped me out."

A small smile tugged at Kamari's lips. "Tegan, huh? I might like her after all." She paused, her eyes searching Sage's. "But if you didn't get my letters, what are you here?"

Sage hesitated; the words she had rehearsed a hundred times suddenly lost. She looked down, tracing the faded graffiti carved into the table by countless visitors before her.

Finally, she raised her head, her eyes locking with Kamari's. "I should be the one—"

"Shut up," Kamari interrupted her tone suddenly sharp and commanding. Her eyes darted to the camera mounted on the ceiling, a silent reminder of the ever-present surveillance. "Whatever you're about to say, just shut up."

Sage blinked, taken aback by the intensity in Kamari's voice. But she quickly understood; they were being recorded, and any misplaced words could have dire consequences. She nodded slightly, acknowledging the unspoken warning.

"I saw you limping when you came in. What happened?" Kamari asked.

"I was hit by a car, but I'm okay," Sage replied, her tone nonchalant, as if trying to downplay the severity of the incident.

Kamari's eyes narrowed, and her lips tightened into a thin line. Her usually composed demeanor was replaced by simmering anger, as though the news had ignited something deep within her. "Was it an accident or on purpose?" Kamari's voice was low.

In the silence, the truth spoke louder than words ever could. Sage's silence was a confession, a silent acknowledgment of the danger that had been stalking her. "You need to make sure you protect yourself at all times," Kamari warned. The words were both a plea and a command.

Sage nodded slowly, feeling the intensity of Kamari's stare, knowing that her aunt's words were not just advice but a desperate plea for her safety.

Kamari shifted her tone, trying to lift the weight of the conversation. "I would like for you to come to my court trial," Kamari said, her voice unexpectedly vulnerable. "You're all the family I have right now." Her eyes softened, showing a rare glimpse of the vulnerability beneath her hardened exterior.

Sage felt a lump form in her throat, her emotions threatening to overwhelm her. She had always looked up to Kamari, and despite everything that had happened, she couldn't deny the bond they shared.

"I love you, Kamari. Of course, I will be there," Sage replied, her voice filled with sincerity.

"I love you too," Kamari replied.

Chapter 11

Unspoken Truths

Avery tapped her hand on her thigh, her impatience clear as she glanced at the clock. Both she and Dr. McCoy's heads snapped up when the door finally opened, and Nora walked in 30 minutes late, offering hurried apologies. Avery rolled her eyes and shook her head in frustration.

Nora settled into her seat, looking up at Dr. McCoy. "So where were we?"

"Waiting for you," Avery snapped, crossing her arms with apparent irritation. She had taken the bus and was clearly upset that Nora was late.

Sensing the tension in the room, Dr. McCoy cleared his throat and began, "So, how was the day out together?"

Avery laughed bitterly as she looked at her mother. The guilt was clear on Nora's face because she had made zero attempts at spending time with Avery. "Sage got hit by a car, and there has been a lot going on at the casino, and I didn't have time," Nora explained, her voice strained.

Dr. McCoy, noticing the agitation on Avery's face, interjected gently. "My apologies, Nora. I hope Sage is doing okay. Avery, how are you feeling about everything?"

"It feels like there is always going to be something with Sage. The most attention I have gotten from my mother in the past two years is when I was kidnapped or when I was doing badly in school. Maybe if I were a bad kid, she would pay more attention to me," Avery said.

Nora looked at her daughter, guilt tightening its grip on her heart. "The reason I barely pay attention sometimes is because I know you're a smart girl, and you're very independent. I don't have to worry about you."

Avery's eyes filled with tears as she shook her head. "I don't want to be independent. I want my mother. I want to talk to you about my girl stuff and boys. The fact that you don't know that I got my period for the first time last month hurts me."

Nora sat in shock, a single tear escaping her eye as she realized she had missed such an important milestone in her child's life. She reached out for Avery's hand, but Avery abruptly stood up and rushed out of the office. Nora instinctively moved to follow her, but Dr. McCoy gently suggested, "Give her a minute."

Nora sank back onto the couch, leaning her head back as tears rolled down the sides of her face. "How could I have missed this?" she whispered, the weight of her neglect pressing down on her.

Dr. McCoy leaned forward, his tone gentle but firm. "Whatever you're not telling her is only going to keep pushing her away. You may think you're protecting her, but leaving her in the dark will only make her life that much harder."

Nora sat up and looked Dr. McCoy in the eyes, her gaze intense and searching. It felt as though the therapist could see right through her, sensing the turmoil she was desperately trying to conceal. Thoughts raced through Nora's mind. Did Dr. McCoy know something about her? Had Avery said something? Or was Dr. McCoy just that damn good at her job?

Pushing her thoughts aside, Nora quickly stood up and extended a hand. "Thank you, Dr. McCoy," she said, her voice steady despite the whirlwind of emotions inside her.

Dr. McCoy smiled warmly, her eyes filled with understanding. "Take care, Nora. Remember, honesty and communication are key."

Nora nodded, taking the advice to heart. As she left the office, she knew she had a long way to go, but she was determined to face her fears and rebuild her relationship with Avery, one step at a time.

Nora and Avery sat quietly in the car, the silence thick with unspoken words and unresolved tension. They drove an hour and a half out to New Jersey, the landscape gradually changing from urban sprawl to dense, deserted forest. Nora pulled the car to a stop and got out, walking to the trunk without a word. Avery followed, her confusion growing with each step.

"Where are we?" Avery asked, her voice tinged with apprehension.

Nora opened the trunk and handed her a pistol. Avery's hand dropped slightly from the unexpected weight of the gun. She looked at her mother, searching for answers, but Nora simply turned and walked into the forest, carrying a duffle bag.

Avery followed closely behind, watching as Nora set up a makeshift shooting range in a small clearing. Glass bottles were lined up on a fallen tree trunk, glinting in the dappled sunlight.

"I want you to shoot those glass bottles down," Nora said, her voice steady but firm.

"Mom, this is stupid. I am not doing this. Stop trying to turn me into Sage. I am not her," Avery protested, her voice rising with frustration.

Nora's expression softened, but her resolve remained firm. "A box was delivered to the casino with a finger inside it that belongs to Warren," she said, her voice heavy with the weight of the truth. "All this time, I thought I was protecting you by keeping you away and telling you the bare minimum, but it's clear that all I was doing was setting you up to be a victim. That ends today."

"You think teaching me how to shoot is going to save me?" Avery chuckled, a hint of bitterness in her voice.

Nora gently grabbed Avery's shoulder, her eyes filled with concern. "No, but if something happens to me, you and Sage have to protect each other. Veronica is coming for us, and I need you to be ready."

Avery looked down at the gun in her hands, then back up at her mother. "This doesn't change the fact that you don't spend time with me," she said, her voice softer but still tinged with hurt.

Nora sighed, her heart aching at Avery's words. "I know, and I'm sorry. I've let you down in so many ways, but I'm trying to make things right. I want to spend time with you, Avery. I want to be the mother you need. But right now, we have to make sure you're safe. Please, let's focus on this for now, and I promise we'll work on us."

Avery's eyes searched her mother's face, looking for sincerity. She saw the pain and regret in Nora's eyes, and for a moment, she felt a flicker of hope.

"Okay, Mom," Avery said quietly. "I'll do this. But you have to promise me that once this is over, things will be different."

Nora nodded, her grip on Avery's shoulder tightening slightly. "I promise, Avery. Things will be different. We'll make it through this together."

Avery faced the glass bottles, gripping the gun tightly. She raised her arm, aiming carefully. Nora stood beside her, adjusting them and whispering words of encouragement.

"Take a deep breath, steady your aim," Nora instructed, her voice calm and reassuring.

Avery squeezed the trigger, but the shot missed its mark. The kickback shook her up a little, but she remembered her mother's words about protecting herself and Sage.

Avery had always been a quiet and shy girl, but holding the gun in her hand made her feel powerful and in control. She took another deep breath and aimed again. This time, her hands were steadier, her resolve stronger.

She fired several more shots, each one inching closer to the target. Finally, one of the bottles shattered, the sound of breaking glass echoing through the forest. A triumphant smile spread across Avery's face.

Nora nodded, her heart swelling with pride and hope. They continued practicing, each shot strengthening Avery's confidence and their bond as they prepared for whatever challenges lay ahead.

***

Sage and Tegan sat on the bleachers overlooking the football field as the sun cast long shadows. "How's your leg?" Tegan asked, glancing at Sage's outstretched limb, still encased in a cast.

"Just a few more days with this cast on, and I can finally go back to playing ball. Maybe," Sage replied, her tone uncertain.

Tegan's eyes widened in surprise. "What do you mean maybe?"

Sage looked out onto the field, her expression contemplative. "I don't know if I want to play basketball anymore."

Tegan frowned, concern etched on her face. "I hope this isn't about Cylus because you are a great ball player, and I know you want to go to the WNBA eventually. Don't let some boy cloud your judgment."

Sage watched the players walking onto the field to practice, the familiar scene stirring mixed emotions. She turned to Tegan, her voice soft but tinged with uncertainty. "Am I stupid for basing my future off of a guy?"

"Absolutely," Tegan laughed. "But we're teenage girls; that's what we do."

Sage wrapped her arm around Tegan, and they embraced, laughing so hard they could barely breathe.

After a moment, Sage pulled back, her expression more serious. "Can I ask you for a favor?"

Tegan's smile faded as she nodded, waiting for Sage to continue.

"Kamari's trial starts tomorrow. Will you come with me?" Sage asked, with uncertainty in her voice.

Tegan's expression turned to one of concern and disinterest, clearly thinking it was a bad idea. Sage turned away, sensing her friend's reluctance.

"She killed Donny, Sage. She doesn't deserve your support. Let that bitch rot," Tegan said, her voice firm and filled with conviction.

Sage took a deep breath, her hands beginning to shake. "I shot someone, and she is taking the fall for it," she confessed, her voice barely above a whisper. She looked at Tegan, her eyes filled with fear. "I'm afraid that she is going to give me up."

Tegan's eyes widened, her face draining of color as she processed Sage's words. For a moment, she was speechless, her mind racing to comprehend the magnitude of the confession. She swallowed hard, trying to find the right words to say.

"You...you shot someone?" Her voice trembled, a mixture of shock and concern. She took a step back, her initial reaction of disbelief giving way to the gravity of the situation. But then, seeing the fear in Sage's eyes, she steeled herself and stepped closer, her hand gently wiping away the single tear that rolled down Sage's cheek.

"Do you think going to the trial is going to change that?" Tegan asked softly, her voice steady despite the whirlwind of emotions inside her.

Sage shrugged her shoulders, feeling the weight of her guilt and uncertainty. "I don't know. Maybe I just need to see it for myself."

Just then, the bell rang, signaling the end of their break. Tegan helped Sage up and handed her the crutches. They slowly walked down the steps of the bleachers, the gravity of Sage's confession hanging heavily in the air. As they made their way back inside the school, Sage felt dread. She knew she had to face the consequences, no matter how terrifying they might be. And despite her initial shock, Tegan's supportive presence gave Sage a small but crucial sense of reassurance.

As Sage and Tegan entered the school building, Cylus accidentally bumped into them. Sage and Cylus made eye contact, and a flicker of recognition and unresolved tension passed between them. He opened his mouth to say something, but the words didn't come out.

Tegan, noticing the awkward silence, rolled her eyes and pulled Sage away. Sage and Cylus continued to look back at each other, the unspoken words hanging in the air as they walked in opposite directions.

Tegan glanced back, noticing the lingering connection between Sage and Cylus. "If it's meant to be, then it will. Until then, focus on yourself. And about going to court, I got you."

Sage smiled, feeling a warmth in Tegan's support. She hugged her tightly. "Thank you, Tegan. I don't know what I'd do without you."

Tegan hugged her back just as tightly. "You'll never have to find out. I'm here for you, always."

Chapter 12

Collision

S age stood outside the courthouse, her heart pounding in her chest. The imposing building loomed above her, its stone facade casting long shadows in the early morning light. She shifted her weight, leaning slightly on her crutches, the cast on her leg a constant reminder of recent events.

Tegan walked up beside her, her presence a comforting anchor in the sea of anxiety that threatened to overwhelm Sage. Without a word, Tegan took Sage's hand, offering silent support. Sage squeezed back, grateful for her friend.

Inside, the courtroom was already filled with people. Sage and Tegan crept to the back, finding seats where they could observe without drawing too much attention. Sage glanced around, her nerves jangling with every whispered conversation and rustle of papers.

Sage stared at the door, her eyes fixed and unblinking, waiting for Kamari to walk out. Her impatience grew with each passing second, her mind racing with thoughts of what was to come. Finally, the doors swung open with a heavy thud, and Sage's breathing quickened, her chest rising and falling rapidly. Tegan, sensing her distress, held her hand tightly.

Kamari walked into the courtroom, her presence commanding and almost surreal. Despite having been in jail for the past few months, she appeared untouched by the harshness of her surroundings. In fact, she seemed to be glowing, her skin radiant, and her posture was confident.

Kamari, bound by two guards, was escorted to her seat at the front of the courtroom. Her eyes scanned the room, taking in every detail. As she settled into her chair, she spotted Nora entering the courtroom. Their eyes met for a brief moment before Kamari's gaze shifted to Sage.

Nora, noticing Sage and Tegan in the back, made her way over and sat down next to them. Sage swallowed hard, and the tension in her body was evident. Nora leaned in and whispered in her ear, "We will talk about this later."

Kamari, noticing the interaction, gave a slight, knowing wink to both Nora and Sage.

Judge Percy, known for his strict demeanor and no-nonsense approach, took his seat at the bench. His sharp, piercing eyes scanned the courtroom, commanding immediate respect and attention. His robes, impeccably pressed, added to his authoritative presence. His voice, deep and unwavering, echoed through the room as he began his opening remarks.

"Members of the jury," Judge Percy began, his tone firm and clear, "Your duty is to impartially consider the evidence presented in this courtroom and render a verdict based solely on the facts and the law. You must follow the legal standards I will provide, setting aside any personal biases or preconceived notions. The responsibility before you is immense, and I expect each of you to uphold the integrity of this court."

He paused, allowing his words to sink in, his gaze unwavering as he continued to address the jury. The silence in the courtroom was palpable, the weight of his expectations pressing down on everyone present.

"The defendant, Kamari Missy Willis, is charged with the following: second-degree murder of Quandel Robinson-Segan, known as Que; second-degree murder of Donny Layfette; assault and reckless endangerment at the Onyx Sabre Casino; and first-degree murder of Crystal Horns by administering a fatal dose of fentanyl. How does the defendant plead?" Judge Percy's voice was steady, each word pronounced with precision and gravity.

Alexandra Sterling stood beside Kamari, her reputation as the best defense attorney in New York preceding her.

"Not guilty, Your Honor," she declared, her voice steady and commanding.

Judge Percy nodded curtly. "Very well. We will now proceed with the opening statements. The prosecution may begin."

The prosecutor, Jacob Matthews, rose from his seat and approached the jury with confident strides. Jacob was known for his fierce determination and unyielding pursuit of justice. His presence was commanding, and as he began his opening statement, the room fell silent, every eye fixed on him.

"Ladies and gentlemen of the jury," Jacob began, his voice strong and clear, "what you will hear over the course of this trial is a story of cold-blooded murder, manipulation, and a callous disregard for human life."

After hours of intense arguments between the attorneys, Judge Percy finally made his closing remarks, setting the date for the continuation of the trial. The courtroom slowly emptied, the weight of the day's proceedings hanging heavily over everyone. Nora dropped Tegan off at her home, and she and Sage drove the rest of the way in silence, each lost in their own thoughts.

As they entered the house, Nora placed her bag on the table and turned to Sage. "Do you want to talk?" she asked, her voice was gentle.

Sage sat down at the table, her shoulders slumped with the weight of her thoughts. "I just wanted to see her. We can't make her go to prison."

Nora sighed, her expression softening as she looked at her daughter. "I'm not upset with you, Sage. I understand why you wanted to see her, but there's nothing I can do about this. She's being charged by the state. She has to do some time."

Sage's eyes filled with frustration and sorrow. "But it's not fair. She's taking the fall for something I did."

Nora reached out, placing a comforting hand on Sage's. "I know it feels unfair, but Kamari's actions are her own. The law sees her as responsible for those crimes. We have to let the legal process play out."

Sage shook her head, tears welling up. "I feel so helpless. Like there's nothing I can do to make it right."

Nora squeezed her hand gently. "If I could, I would help, but we have more important matters to deal with. Right now, we need to focus on protecting ourselves and each other."

"What's more important than getting your sister out of jail?" Sage demanded, her frustration boiling over.

"She committed a crime, Sage," Nora replied, her voice rising slightly.

Sage slammed her fist on the table, making the dishes rattle. "So did we!"

At that moment, Avery walked into the kitchen, her eyes wide with confusion. Sage turned to her, her voice sharp. "Go back to your room, Avery!"

Nora held up a hand, stopping Avery in her tracks. "No, stay. Avery is part of this family, and she has the right to know what's going on."

Avery looked between them, her confusion deepening. "What's happening?"

Sage took a deep breath, her anger still simmering but controlled. "You need to talk to Detective Douglas and see what he can do to help Kamari," she said, turning back to Nora. "If not..."

Nora and Avery looked at Sage, waiting for her to finish her sentence. The tension in the room was palpable.

"If not, I am going to turn myself in. I can't let her take the fall for Que's murder," Sage said, her voice trembling.

"Are you crazy?" Avery asked, her eyes wide with shock.

"I love you, Avery, but please stay out of this. It does not concern you," Sage responded, her voice softening but still firm.

"My sister is talking about turning herself in for murder, and it's not my concern?" Avery shot back, her voice rising with emotion.

"Fine. I will speak to Douglas and see what can be done but don't get your hopes up because she has to do time. Maybe the length can be changed," Nora said, her voice heavy with resignation.

Avery's face twisted in confusion. "She killed Donny," she choked out, tears welling up in her eyes. "Why would y'all want to help her?"

Sage's expression hardened. "You're a child. You wouldn't understand," she said dismissively.

Avery's eyes narrowed, anger flaring up. "And what are you? You think because you pulled a trigger that makes you grown?" she retorted, rolling her eyes.

Sage stood up, the tension between them escalating. She walked up to Avery, her posture challenging. Nora quickly intervened, placing her hand between them to keep them from attacking each other. Sage and Avery locked eyes, a fierce stare-down ensuing. Despite the tension, Avery stood her ground, refusing to back down.

"Alright, enough of this," Nora said firmly, her voice cutting through the tension. "Y'all are sisters. Remember that."

Avery smirked as Sage walked away to her room. Nora lightly slapped her on the back of her head. "Why do you antagonize her?"

"I just think it's crazy that you all want to help Kamari after everything. On top of you dealing with this casino thing. I know you wish you could have been there for her, but there are other ways to help."

Nora was impressed with Avery's maturity about the situation. "When did you become so wise?"

"Well, I am turning 13 in two weeks. It might be old age," Avery quipped, and both of them laughed before embracing each other.

Just then, Nora's phone buzzed with a text message. She glanced at the screen, and her expression immediately turned serious. "There's a problem at the casino. I need to go."

Chapter 13

Hostile Takeover

Nora walked into the office where Luke and Benjamin were seated, both looking over some papers with intense concentration. She placed her bag on the table, her eyes narrowing as she took in their serious expressions. "What's the problem?" she asked, her voice firm.

Benjamin looked up with frustration in his eyes. "We found out who has been skimming profits."

Nora's eyebrows shot up. "Who?"

"Stephanie Ryde," Benjamin said, pointing to a report on the table. "She's at poker table two right now."

Nora's jaw tightened as she processed the information. Stephanie had always seemed trustworthy, but clearly, appearances could be deceiving. She turned to Luke, who was frowning at the papers in front of him.

"What's our move?" Nora asked, her voice low and serious.

Luke looked up, meeting her gaze. "We need to confront her, but we have to be careful. We don't want to cause a scene that could tip her off or disrupt the casino."

Nora nodded, agreeing with his assessment. "Alright, let's handle this discreetly. Benjamin, do we have enough evidence to prove she's the one skimming?"

Benjamin nodded, tapping the papers on the table. "Yes, I've cross-checked the numbers and the surveillance footage. It all points to her."

Nora looked through the glass down at the bustling casino floor, her eyes tracking Stephanie as she moved around the slot machines and poker tables. Stephanie was a woman in her mid-30s with a sharp bob haircut, perfectly manicured nails, and an air of confidence that bordered on arrogance. She wore a sleek black dress that hugged her figure, accessorized with understated but elegant jewelry. Despite her polished exterior, there was an edge to her demeanor, a hint of something calculating beneath the surface.

Nora picked up the phone and made a call to security. "Escort Stephanie Ryde to my office," she instructed, her voice calm but firm.

Moments later, the door to the office opened, and Stephanie walked in, her smile bright but her eyes wary. Nora gestured for Benjamin to leave, and he nodded, gathering his papers and exited the room. Luke stood up, allowing Nora to take his place across from Stephanie.

"Have a seat," Nora said, her tone leaving no room for argument.

Stephanie sat down, crossing her legs and maintaining her smile. "How are you?" she asked, her voice sweet but with a hint of apprehension.

Nora's face was serious, as unwavering as a granite statue. "Let's cut the formalities. You've been here since this casino opened, so I know you know the protocol for how money is deposited." She intertwined her fingers on the table, her gaze never leaving Stephanie's. "You've been coming up short."

Stephanie's smile faltered slightly, but she quickly recovered, trying to maintain her composure. "I don't know what you're talking about, Nora. There must be some mistake."

Nora leaned forward, her eyes narrowing. "No mistake, Stephanie. We have the records, the surveillance footage, and the discrepancies all point to you. This is your chance to come clean."

"I swear I am not stealing any money. Don't fire me," Stephanie pleaded, her voice breaking. "I need this job. I have children."

Nora's expression remained stern. "So do I, and when your money comes up short, you take food out of my children's mouths. So tell us the truth."

Before Stephanie could respond, the door swung open, and Veronica stood in the doorway, flanked by a group of imposing men. She stepped in confidently, her presence commanding the room. "Stephanie, close your mouth," Veronica ordered, her voice cold and authoritative.

Stephanie's demeanor shifted instantly. The fear in her eyes was replaced by a sly smile as she glanced back at Nora and Luke. It became clear to them that Stephanie and Veronica were working together.

Nora and Veronica locked eyes, the tension between them palpable. "I remember what I said the last time we spoke because I was there when I said it. Two weeks have come and gone."

"Where is Warren?" Nora asked, her voice edged with desperation.

Veronica walked around the desk, closing the distance between them until she stood directly in front of Nora. "You don't ask me shit. You lost that opportunity when you didn't sign over the papers. The next box I send you will have his head inside."

She paused, her gaze never wavering. "Clearly, me giving you time to get your affairs in order did nothing. So, you know what?" She placed a pen on the desk with a sharp click. "I am here to sign the papers. I'm done waiting."

Nora and Luke exchanged a tense glance. There had been no one in Nora's life who made her fear them, but there was something about Veronica that sent shivers down her spine.

"That's not how this works," Nora said, trying to keep her voice steady. "There are a lot of legalities that go into it."

Veronica's eyes narrowed, her patience wearing thin. "I don't want to hear that bullshit. I have given you all two weeks to get the legalities in order, and you did nothing. This is a hostile takeover. You are clearly having financial struggles with all these discrepancies. The shareholders aren't too pleased."

"Well, until the shareholders get in contact with us, you aren't getting shit. Build your own damn casino!" Luke yelled.

Veronica's smile widened as she placed her bag on the table. With deliberate slowness, she pulled out a gun, a silencer already attached to the barrel. She stared at Nora, her eyes cold and unyielding, and then, without a word, she raised the gun and pulled the trigger. The shot was muffled, but the impact was immediate. Stephanie's body jerked violently as the bullet hit her temple, and she crumpled to the floor.

Nora took a heavy breath, her face contorted with rage and horror. She felt a wave of nausea but forced herself to stay composed, knowing any sign of weakness would only embolden Veronica further.

Veronica's eyes never left Nora's as she spoke, her voice calm and unbothered. "The shareholders will be in contact with you this week." She walked over to Stephanie's lifeless body and stepped over her without a hint of remorse. "You might want to clean this up."

With that, she turned and walked out of the office, her men following close behind. The door closed with a heavy thud, leaving Nora and Luke in stunned silence.

Chapter 14

Unraveling

Mylan and Sarah were in the bathroom, as Mylan showered and Sarah was putting on makeup. "You need to call your sister," Sarah said, her tone insistent.

Mylan screamed over the sound of the running water. "I don't have time for her childish ass."

Sarah pulled back the shower curtain, her head cocked to the side. "That's your sister, and you know she is dealing with a lot with Warren getting taken by Veronica."

She walked back to the mirror, continuing to apply her makeup. Mylan turned off the shower, grabbing a towel. "What the hell do you mean Warren was taken? By who? How do you even know? You've been talking to my sister?"

She took a deep breath. "Calm down. Of course, we have been speaking. I don't have an issue with her. You need to get over this Luke thing because you are going to lose her again. Maybe you might be right about him, but that's something she will have to figure out for herself." She ran her fingers through her strawberry blonde hair, the soft waves framing her face perfectly.

She took a deep breath. "Calm down. Of course, we have been speaking. I don't have an issue with her. You need to get over this Luke thing because you are going to lose her again. Maybe you might be right about him, but that's something she will have to figure out for herself." She ran her fingers through her strawberry blonde hair, the soft waves framing her face perfectly.

"That's the thing. I don't want her to figure it out when it's too late." He stood behind her and wrapped his arms around her waist as they both looked at each other in the mirror. "I will call her."

He kissed her on the cheek and stepped out of the bathroom. She smiled at him as he walked away. "I love you, baby," she said, admiring the view of his back.

"I love you too," Mylan replied, glancing back with a reassuring smile.

***

Sarah and Avery walked through the park, and the gentle sounds of birds chirping and children playing created a peaceful backdrop. Baby Laverne sat contentedly in the stroller, her tiny hands gripping a soft toy.

"How has therapy been going with your mother?" Sarah asked, her eyes warm with concern.

"It's been okay," Avery replied, her voice thoughtful. "I feel like I can finally say what's on my mind. I even told her that I got my period." Avery paused, looking down at her feet as they walked. "She seemed hurt that I didn't tell her."

Sarah smiled with empathy in her expression. "I'm glad you finally told her. I did expect her to be hurt about it, but now she knows how you feel, and hopefully, things will get better. It takes time, but at least you both are on the same page."

Avery nodded, a hint of a smile playing on her lips. "Yeah, I hope so. It feels good to be honest with her finally."

Sarah glanced at Avery, her tone gentle. "It's a big step, and I'm proud of you. Communication is key, even if it's hard sometimes. Your mom loves you, and she wants to be there for you."

Avery looked up, her eyes reflecting a glimmer of hope. "I know. I just wish things weren't so complicated."

Sarah sighed, her thoughts drifting to Mylan and Nora. "I understand. I'm just hoping that Mylan and Nora will speak to each other soon. It's tough when family members don't see eye to eye."

Avery took the stroller from Sarah, her hands gripping the handle tightly. "I'm with Uncle Mylan about Luke.

Something just doesn't seem right. He is love-bombing Mom, and she doesn't even see it. Like, this engagement is ridiculous. They barely know each other."

Sarah's expression shifted to one of concern. Her eyebrows furrowed slightly, and she bit her lower lip as she processed Avery's words. Her usually warm eyes took on a more serious, thoughtful look, and she sighed deeply before speaking.

"You have clearly thought a lot about this, and maybe you might be right, but it is not your place—"

"Yeah, yeah, yeah, I know. Stay in a child's place, but you know I'm right," Avery interjected, rolling her eyes.

Sarah wanted to change the topic to something more positive and asked about Sage. Avery rolled her eyes, clearly frustrated. "Everything is still all about Sage. Sometimes, I feel like she does things to get all the attention to herself."

"So you think she purposely stepped in front of the car to get hit? You think Cylus broke up with her so that she could get attention?" Sarah's voice was calm, but her question was pointed.

Avery stopped walking, turning sharply to face Sarah. "Maybe we're both selfish brats that only think about ourselves. I wanted the attention to be on me so much that I never stopped to ask her how she was feeling."

Sarah stepped closer, her tone softening. "It's okay to feel like you want attention, too, Avery. Everyone needs to feel seen and heard. But it's also important to remember that everyone is dealing with their own struggles."

Avery sighed heavily, her shoulders slumping. "I know. I just... it's hard. I miss the way things used to be before everything got so complicated." She blinked back tears. "I guess I should talk to Sage. Really talk to her, and not just about me."

"That sounds like a good idea," Sarah said with a warm smile. "I'm sure she'd appreciate it. Sometimes, just knowing that someone cares can make a big difference."

Avery gave Sarah a big hug. "You always know what to say." Sarah embraced Avery and kissed her on the cheek.

They continued to walk, enjoying the peaceful moment, until baby Laverne started to cry. Avery stopped pushing the stroller and kneeled down in front of her, making silly faces to get her to stop crying. Laverne let out a big chuckle, her tears quickly forgotten.

Sarah's smile slowly turned into a frown as a man dressed in all black walked up to them. His face was partially obscured by a hood, and his eyes were cold and hard. He held a gun up to Sarah. "Gimme all ya money," the man demanded, his voice low and threatening.

Avery stood up, her grip tightening on the stroller. "Please, we don't have anything," she said, her voice trembling.

The man's eyes darted to the stroller, then back to Sarah. "I'm not gonna ask again," he growled, waving the gun slightly for emphasis.

Sarah's heart raced, and she slowly raised her hands, trying to stay calm. "Okay, okay, just stay calm. Let me get my purse." She reached for her bag, her hands shaking.

Avery glanced at Laverne, who was now silent, sensing the tension. "Please, don't hurt us," Avery pleaded, her eyes wide with fear.

Sarah handed over her purse, trying to keep her movements slow and non-threatening. The man grabbed it and rifled through it quickly, his expression frustrated when he found only a small amount of cash.

"Please, we don't want no trouble," Avery said, her voice trembling.

"Am I talking to you, little girl?" he yelled, his voice echoed with anger.

The man threw Sarah's purse back at her, its contents scattering across the ground. "Broke bitch. Where's the rest of it? I know you have more."

Avery, her hands shaking, took out fifty dollars her mother had given her earlier that day. She handed it to him. "Just take the money and go."

Frustrated with Avery speaking, the man slapped her across the face. Avery stumbled and fell to the ground, her cheek stinging from the impact. Sarah immediately moved to help her, but before she could reach Avery, she felt the cold barrel of the gun pressed against her temple.

"Please, don't shoot," Sarah pleaded, her voice breaking.

Her words were ignored as the man pulled the trigger. The gunshot rang out, and Sarah's body dropped instantly.

Avery's eyes widened, her pupils dilating in terror. She clutched the grass beneath her, her breathing rapid and shallow. She used all of her strength to stand up, her legs shaky but determined. She reached under her shirt and pulled out the small handgun her mother had insisted she carry for protection. With a quick, instinctive motion, she aimed at the man as he turned to flee. Her hand steadied, and she squeezed the trigger. The shot rang out, hitting the man squarely in the arm. He stumbled, clutching his wound, but managed to escape into the shadows of the park.

Avery wrapped the gun in the baby clothes from the stroller, her movements hurried but precise and shoved it into the baby bag. Her heart pounded as she grabbed her phone and dialed 911.

Chapter 15

Breaking Point

Nora, Sage, Avery, and baby Laverne were in the hospital waiting room. It felt like they practically lived there, always finding themselves back in those sterile, fluorescent-lit halls, as if the hospital was their second home. Avery sat staring into space, her eyes bloodshot and her clothes covered in Sarah's blood.

Mylan walked into the waiting room, his steps brisk and purposeful. "Where's Sarah?" he asked, his voice lacking the fear or worry one might expect. It was almost like he knew Sarah was okay like he had some unspoken assurance. Nobody answered him. "What room is she in?"

He quickly noticed Avery covered in blood, tears streaming down her face. Baby Laverne slept peacefully in her stroller, oblivious to the chaos around her. Mylan's eyes darted to Sage, who sat utterly mute, her face pale and expressionless. Finally, he turned to Nora, who looked back at him with a pained expression.

"Nora," his voice lowered, thick with dread. "Where's my wife?"

Nora gently placed her hand on Mylan's arm. "Mylan, let's step outside for a moment," she urged, her voice soft yet insistent.

Mylan pulled away from her grasp, his eyes wild with desperation. "Where is Sarah?" he demanded again, his voice rising in panic.

Nora took a deep breath, her own eyes filling with tears. "I'm so sorry, Mylan. She didn't make it. Sarah's gone." She repeated the words, trying to make him understand, each "sorry" like a dagger to her own heart.

Mylan's face twisted in agony as the truth sunk in, his breathing growing ragged. Sensing the explosion of grief and anger about to erupt, Nora grabbed his arm firmly and dragged him outside the hospital. He resisted at first but eventually allowed himself to be led through the automatic doors and into the cool night air.

Still, inside the waiting room, Sage turned to face Avery and kneeled down in front of her. "Tell me what happened."

Avery's body shook uncontrollably, her eyes wide and unblinking. The tears streamed down her cheeks, seemingly endless. "I shot him," she whispered, her voice barely audible.

Sage felt her heart crumble inside her chest. She gently took Avery's trembling hands, the weight of the situation pressing down on her. She had never wanted Avery to experience the horror of pulling a trigger. Sage had to think quickly. "Where's the gun?"

Avery's eyes flicked down to the baby bag in the stroller. Sage followed her gaze and nodded. She took a napkin from her pocket and gently wiped Avery's tear-streaked face. "We need to get out of here and get rid of the gun," she whispered urgently.

Avery nodded, her movements stiff and mechanical. They stood up, trying to appear as calm as possible. Just as they were about to leave the waiting room, Detective Douglas walked in, his eyes scanning the room before landing on them.

Sage was relieved to see Detective Douglas. Before she could say anything, he gave them a look, almost a warning not to say anything. Just then, Detective Matthew walked in, his expression one of disdain. "It's always something with this family," Matthew muttered, his eyes narrowing as he pulled out his notepad and began to scribble.

Douglas quickly stepped in. "We can't question minors without a guardian present, Matthew. You know that."

Nora walked back in without Mylan, her eyes darting between the detectives and her daughters. "Officers, how may I help you?"

Matthew looked up from his notepad, a slight smirk playing on his lips. "Actually, we should be asking how we can help you. Somebody wants you and your family dead."

Nora's face hardened. "Then you need to go after Veronica Segan," she demanded. "Instead of questioning my daughters."

Matthew's smirk faded as he glanced at Douglas, who remained silent but watchful. "We're doing our job, ma'am. We need to understand what happened."

Nora turned to Sage and Avery, her voice firm but gentle. "Bring baby Laverne. We're leaving."

Douglas nodded slightly, his eyes meeting Nora's briefly in a silent understanding. "Just be careful," he murmured as they walked past.

As they moved toward the exit, Matthew's voice called after them, "This isn't over. We'll be in touch."

Nora didn't respond; she focused solely on getting her family out of the hospital.

***

Avery sat on the bathroom toilet as Sage gently cleaned her face, removing the blood splatter that had dried on her skin. Avery remained quiet, the weight of the night's events pressing down on her. As the realization of Sarah's death settled in, tears began to stream down her cheeks. Sage quickly wrapped her arms around her, holding her tightly.

"Everything is going to be okay," Sage whispered, trying to soothe her sister.

"No, it's not," Avery replied, her voice barely audible. "I couldn't protect her. I thought that if I was able to use a gun, I could help someone, but I froze. I should have shot him first."

Sage took a deep breath, her heart aching for Avery. "Avery, you did what you could. You shouldn't even be involved in any of this. The last thing I ever wanted was for you to have to resort to shooting someone. That's not who you are."

Avery looked up, her eyes filled with pain and confusion. "Is that who you are?"

Sage paused, her hands still holding the cloth stained with Avery's tears and blood. She sighed deeply, her eyes reflecting a sadness and weariness far beyond her years. "What I've done does not define who I am. Yes, I made mistakes, and I am going to continue making them, but I am not allowing those things to dictate who I am, and neither should you."

"I'm sorry," Avery said, her voice barely a whisper.

"Sorry about what?" Sage's brow furrowed, her lips parting slightly in confusion. Her eyes searched Avery's face for answers.

"I never checked in on you when Dad died, the kidnapping, Mom... the drugs. I've been so selfish, always upset about the attention being on you, that I never stopped to think if you even wanted it."

Sage helped her undress, moving with gentle care. "I'm the big sister. I should be checking on you. But I'm fine."

Avery paused, her eyes locking onto Sage with an intensity that spoke volumes. "Were you fine when you were on drugs?" They stared at one another, the air thick with unspoken emotions. Avery's eyes softened, showing warmth and caring that reached deep into Sage's heart. "Why did you do it?"

Sage smiled, but there was no happiness behind her eyes. "Don't worry about me. I am doing better now. No drugs, no alcohol. Nothing. I am okay, and the only thing that's important to me right now is making sure that you get through this."

Avery wrapped her arms around Sage's neck. "I love you." Sage hugged her back. "I love you more."

Sage helped her into the shower, adjusting the water temperature and making sure Avery was comfortable. "I'll come back to check on you in a minute." She gave Avery a reassuring nod before stepping out of the bathroom.

Once in her bedroom, Sage closed the door and leaned back against it. The weight of everything they had been through finally overwhelmed her. She crouched down, and tears began to hit the floor. She covered her mouth with her hand to stifle her sobs, not wanting Avery to hear her cries.

She rushed over to her dresser and started digging through the drawers. "Where is it?" she whispered to herself, desperation in her voice. Clothes flew everywhere as she rummaged through her closet. Finally, she opened a small purse and found a small bag of cocaine inside.

Sage sat on her bed, holding the bag in her trembling hand. She opened it and stared at the powder, her mind racing. The temptation was overwhelming. She glanced over at her phone, then took it up and made a call. "Hey, meet me at Joe's Pizza in 30."

Before leaving, she took a deep breath and made a decision. Sage walked into the bathroom, opened the bag, and flushed the cocaine down the toilet. She made sure Avery was tucked in bed before leaving the apartment. She quietly closed the door behind her and headed out into the night.

****

Sage sat at the wooden square table, her eyes distant as she stared into space. The pizza spot, Joe's Pizza, was the only 24-hour pizza joint in Brooklyn, a haven for late-night workers and partygoers seeking solace in a slice of greasy goodness. The aroma of baking dough and melting cheese filled the air, mingling with the hum of the neon sign outside and the occasional chatter of customers.

She looked up when she heard the bell above the door ring as it opened. A smile spread across her face as she saw Emily, Jenna, and Alex walk in. The sober crew had arrived.

"I know you only called me, but you sounded like you needed more support, so I invited Alex and Jenna. Hope that's okay," Emily said, her eyes full of concern.

"You were right. I do need support right now," Sage admitted, her voice barely above a whisper. "I ordered a cheese pizza already."

They all sat down, and the table went silent for a moment, the gravity of the situation settling in. The warmth and light of the pizza place seemed a stark contrast to the turmoil Sage felt inside.

"We've missed you at the program. Where have you been?" Emily asked, breaking the silence, her tone gentle but probing.

Sage looked down at her hands as they began to shake uncontrollably. Emily reached over and held her hand. "Whatever it is, you can tell us." Alex and Jenna nodded in agreement.

"My aunt was killed today in a robbery," Sage whispered, her voice trembling.

Emily, Alex, and Jenna exchanged glances, unsure what to say. "I am so sorry, Sage," Jenna said softly.

"That's awful," Alex added. "Did they catch who did it?"

Sage shook her head, tears rolling down her face.

They paused as the waitress brought the pizza, but no one was in the mood to eat. The pizza sat untouched in the middle of the table, a silent testament to the gravity of the moment.

Emily handed Sage a napkin to wipe her tears. "Did you use?" she asked gently.

Sage took a deep breath. "I was going to, but then I called you."

Emily squeezed her hand. "That's a big step, Sage. Reaching out instead of using."

"I know there's not much we can do or say to make you feel better, but you took a big step calling someone," Alex added, trying to see the positive in the tragedy.

Jenna and Emily agreed, smiling encouragingly at Sage. She began to share some memories about Sarah with the sober crew, careful to navigate the complex family history. Despite the heavy atmosphere, the crew continued to share stories and laughs, their camaraderie a small but powerful comfort.

It was getting late, and Jenna and Alex eventually left, offering hugs and promises to check in soon. Sage and Emily remained at the table, the pizza now cold, but their spirits somewhat lifted.

"I remember when you first came to the program, you talked a lot about another aunt of yours," Emily said, her curiosity piqued. "You said you had a close relationship with her. Where is she? Are you still close with her?"

"Kamari... she's in jail," Sage said, glancing at Emily and noticing her shift in her seat. "She did something bad, and now she has to pay for it, but no, we aren't close anymore."

Emily took a deep breath. "My mom's in prison for life." She swallowed hard. "She killed my father... because he touched me."

Sage's eyes widened, her heart aching for Emily. "I am so sorry that happened to you."

"I've come a long way, but I am better now, and this program has helped me a lot," Emily said, her voice steady but tinged with lingering pain. "I only told you that because I've always been close with my mom. I talk to her every other day, and I see her at least twice a month. If you and your aunt Kamari were as close as my mother and I are, then I'm sure she would like to hear from you or even see you."

Sage had thought about it a million times, about going to the jailhouse, especially after seeing Kamari in the courtroom. All she wanted was to hug her again, to feel the comforting embrace that once provided her with a sense of safety and love. But the love Sage had for Kamari was overshadowed by her aunt's evil ways and the darkness that had infiltrated their lives.

She looked down at her hands, the urge to reach out almost palpable. Emily's words resonated with her, but the fear and anger were still strong. Kamari had made choices that had torn their family apart, and despite the yearning to reconnect, there was a barrier Sage couldn't seem to cross.

Chapter 16

The Calm Before

The next day at Mylan's condo, Nora, Avery, and Sage were cleaning up while Mylan sat with baby Laverne in the back room. The air was thick with unspoken tension, each of them lost in their thoughts as they went about their tasks.

"Ma, what are we going to do?" Sage asked, breaking the silence. "Veronica is not going to stop, and I know you're trying to do the right thing by letting the police handle it, but we gotta fight back."

Just then, Mylan walked into the kitchen, and they stopped talking, their eyes darting to him cautiously. No one knew what Mylan's state of mind was, but behind those dead eyes screamed rage. He moved with a quiet intensity, his jaw clenched and his movements precise.

Without a word, Mylan pushed back the couch and lifted the carpet, revealing a hidden trapdoor. He opened it to reveal a small arsenal of weapons and contraptions. Guns, knives, grenades, and various tools of defense and offense were neatly arranged, a stark reminder of the lengths he was willing to go to protect his family.

Nora stepped forward, her eyes widening in shock. "What is your plan? Walk up to her home and start throwing grenades? Are you crazy?"

"My wife is dead. Our child is almost a one-year-old baby, and my wife is dead." His voice cracked. "What am I supposed to tell her? Huh? When she asks about her mother, what am I supposed to tell her?" He wiped his tears with his shirt and roughly sat on the sofa, his body shaking with grief.

Nora signaled for Avery and Sage to give them privacy. Once they were gone, she knelt beside Mylan, her eyes filled with empathy and sorrow. "You tell her that her mother saved Aunt Nora's life. You tell her that Sarah was an amazing nurse and was studying to be a neurologist. She was a wonderful wife and an even better mother. That's what you tell her."

Mylan wiped his tears before they could fall, his hands trembling. "I called her father. No answer. He didn't even show up to the hospital. I guess being a police captain is more important than identifying your daughter's body."

"Captain? What's his name?" Nora questioned.

"Max. Max Langford," Mylan replied as he stood up and walked towards the fridge, needing a moment to gather himself.

Nora's mind began racing, remembering that Langford was Douglas's captain. "Oh shit," she muttered, the pieces starting to fall into place.

Mylan turned to look at her, noticing the concern etched on her face. "What is it? What are you thinking?"

She took a deep breath and explained her suspicions. "Mylan, Langford is Douglas's captain. If he's under Veronica's influence, that could explain why he didn't come to the hospital. It makes sense now—why Douglas's investigation keeps getting shut down."

Mylan's eyes narrowed as he processed this information. "So, you think Langford is working for Veronica? That's why he didn't show up to identify Sarah's body?"

Nora nodded, her expression serious. "It's possible. If Langford is in Veronica's pocket, then he's compromised. It means we can't trust the police to handle this. We have to be even more careful."

Mylan clenched his fists, his anger bubbling to the surface. "That bitch. She's got her claws everywhere."

Sage and Avery came back into the kitchen just as a knock sounded at the door. They all glanced at the hidden weapons, the sudden tension in the room palpable.

Mylan reached behind his back and pulled out the gun tucked into his waistband, his eyes narrowing with determination. Nora and Sage quickly picked up pistols from Warren's stash, their hands steady despite the rush of adrenaline. Avery, still new to the world of violence but ready to protect her family, grabbed a taser.

Nora slowly walked over to the door and quickly looked through the peephole. She took a breath and opened the door. Celine was standing there, smiling, but her expression quickly changed when she saw everyone armed. She closed the door behind her. "What the hell did I just walk into? Are you all preparing for World War 3?"

"What are you doing here?" Nora asked, her voice tense.

Mylan stepped forward. "I called her over," he blurted out. He gave Celine a hug, and she comforted him, sensing the gravity of the situation.

Celine nodded, taking a moment to absorb the seriousness of the atmosphere. "I have an idea of where she might be keeping Warren. That's first on the agenda." She pulled out a map and spread it across the table. "This is Veronica's mansion. She has a secret room built directly under her bedroom." She pointed to a spot on the map that wasn't on the original floor plan. "All we have to do is get him out of there."

"You say that like it's easy. She has that whole place locked down with security," Sage said, her voice tinged with frustration. "And how do you even know Warren is down there? How close are you with this woman?"

Celine took a deep breath. "Because I've been there. Every now and then, I provide her with girls for her parties. It just so happens she has one tomorrow night, and I need a new girl."

Nora's eyes widened in disbelief. "Are you asking me to pimp out my daughter? Even if the thought crossed my mind, she knows what Sage looks like."

"She doesn't know Avery," Mylan added quietly.

"Hell no!" Nora yelled, her voice echoing through the room. "She is only 12. I will not use either one of them as bait. That shit never works."

Celine raised her hands in a calm gesture. "I get it, Nora. But listen, this might be our only chance to get in without raising suspicion. We can disguise Avery to make her look older. She doesn't have to do anything. Just get in and create a distraction."

Nora shook her head vehemently. "No. We'll find another way. I will not put my daughters in that kind of danger."

Mylan stepped closer to Nora, his voice calm but firm. "Nora, I understand your concern. But this might be our best shot. We'll all be there, ready to move in as soon as she's inside. It's risky, but every plan we come up with will be risky."

Avery, who had been silent up until now, stepped forward. "Mom, I want to help. I can do this. I'm not a little kid anymore. If it means getting Warren back, I'll do it."

"What's the other option?" Nora asked, her voice filled with frustration.

Celine sighed and explained, "The other options require an army, which we don't have, and there's nobody bold enough to go up against Veronica Segan."

"Let's say we go through with your plan, and we get Warren. Then what? We're still going to be in the same position," Nora countered, her tone edged with skepticism.

"But at least Warren would be with us," Sage interjected, her voice steady and firm. "We can't just leave him there. We have to do something."

Celine nodded and added, "Look, I also provide bottle service at these parties. Avery only has to serve bottles. That's it. I'll be watching her the entire time. If it becomes too much, I can pull her out immediately."

Nora took a deep breath, feeling the weight of the decision pressing down on her. She looked around the room, seeing the resolve in her family's eyes. "Alright," she said, her voice trembling slightly. "We go through with the plan. But we need to be ready for anything."

Mylan nodded, though his expression was still troubled. "We'll get Warren out first. Then we can figure out our next move."

Celine pulled out the map again and spread it on the table. "Here's the plan. Avery, you'll go in with me as part of the bottle service. Sage, Mylan, and Nora, you'll be outside, ready to move in if anything goes wrong. We need to stay in constant communication."

Mylan looked at the map, his eyes scanned every detail. "What about an exit? Once we get Warren, how do we get out without alerting everyone?"

Celine pointed to a back entrance on the map. "There's a back exit here. It's not heavily guarded, and it leads to the woods behind the mansion. We'll use that to get out quickly."

Nora nodded, her mind racing with the logistics. "We'll need a distraction to cover our escape. Something that will draw the guards away from us."

"I can handle that," Mylan said, his voice steady. "I'll set off a small explosion away from the mansion. That should give us enough time to get out."

Nora looked over at Avery with guilt in her eyes. The weight of her life decisions that had caused her daughters to be put in these situations pressed heavily on her heart. She started to rethink every choice, every moment that had led them here. With a deep, shuddering breath, she glanced at Sage and pulled both of her daughters into a tight embrace.

Tears filled her eyes as she whispered, "I'm sorry," her voice choked with emotion. "I'm so, so sorry."

Chapter 17

Lion's Den

Nora and Luke were seated in the car on the main street behind Veronica's mansion, the tension in the air palpable as they waited in silence.

"I just don't understand why I was not included in making this plan," Luke complained, breaking the silence. He shifted in his seat, clearly frustrated.

Nora shook her head in annoyance, her patience wearing thin. "Does it matter? You're here now."

"How do you even know this Celine girl? And how do you know you can trust her?" Luke pressed, his voice rising with irritation.

But Nora was more concerned about Avery and what was going on inside that mansion. Her mind raced with possibilities, each more frightening than the last, and she found it hard to focus on anything else.

"Are you not listening to me? Tell me what the hell is going on?" Luke yelled, his voice echoing in the confines of the car.

"Shut up!" she screamed, her voice cutting through the night. "My daughter is in there and could possibly be in danger. I don't give a damn about what you have to say right now. You back me up when it's time to back me up. Period." Her eyes blazed with intensity, leaving no room for argument.

Luke sat back in the car and crossed his arms, huffing like a little girl who didn't get her way. His pouting was almost comical, but Nora didn't have the patience for it right now.

"Come on," Nora instructed as she opened the car door, motioning for him to follow her. Reluctantly, Luke got out, still sulking, and joined her as they walked into the dense woods that separated the main street from Veronica's mansion. The crunch of leaves underfoot and the sound of their breathing were the only noises breaking the night's stillness.

Inside the mansion, the atmosphere was buzzing with activity. Celine stood in the kitchen with the other bottle girls, who were busy preparing for the party. Avery, disguised to blend in, wore a sleek black cocktail dress that hugged her slender frame, its hemline just above her knees. Her hair was pulled back into a high ponytail, and her lips were painted a bold red. The dress was elegant but modest, allowing her to move easily while maintaining an air of sophistication.

Though on the inside, Avery was shitting herself, her heart racing with anxiety, on the outside, she remained poised, her expression calm and composed. She took deep breaths, reminding herself to stay focused.

Celine, conducting business as usual, was checking the supplies for the night. "What the fuck is this?" she snapped at one of the girls, pointing to a small tray of cocaine. "This ain't enough coke. Add more."

Avery watched the exchange, trying to appear casual, but Celine caught her standing in the corner, looking tense and out of place. With a knowing look, Celine walked over to her and whispered, "You need to get it together. You're looking like an undercover cop. Relax. Blend in."

Avery nodded, swallowing hard. "Got it," she replied, her voice steady despite her nerves.

Taking a deep breath, Avery straightened her shoulders and joined the other girls, carefully measuring out drinks and chatting as if she belonged. She knew she had to play her part convincingly, not just for herself but for her family waiting outside.

Avery walked out into the living room, where the party was in full swing. The room was filled with men of all statues and wealth, their laughter and conversation blending with the soft strains of jazz music playing in the background. The air was thick with the mingling scents of cigars and expensive cologne.

Avery worked the room like she had been doing it her whole life, gracefully passing out drinks and trays of neatly arranged lines of cocaine, keeping her face neutral and composed. Despite the lavish surroundings, she remained on high alert, her eyes scanning the crowd for any sign of trouble or Warren.

As she maneuvered through the crowd, an older white man suddenly reached out and gripped her ass with a lustful smirk. Avery jumped back, her heart racing with anger and disgust. "Don't touch me," she snapped, her voice steady despite the adrenaline coursing through her veins.

"What you say, bitch?" the man screamed, stumbling forward and knocking the drinks and drugs out of her hands, sending the contents crashing to the ground. The noise drew the attention of the partygoers, and a hush fell over the room as heads turned to watch the commotion unfold.

Celine, who had been watching Avery from a distance, quickly rushed over to defuse the situation. Her presence commanded authority, and she stepped between Avery and the man, her expression fierce. "What's going on?" she demanded, her voice low but firm.

Avery looked up at her, trying to keep her voice steady. "He touched me," she whispered, her anger barely contained.

Celine turned to the man, her eyes cold and unyielding. "Don't touch the bottle girls!" she announced loudly, ensuring everyone in the room heard her. "I am not going to say it twice."

Veronica walked over to inquire about the problem. The man stood up, "I paid you good money and I want what I want and I want her." He pointed to Avery.

Avery swallowed her spit at the thought of that man putting his hands all over her. She looked at Celine, and Celine looked back at her. Veronica looked at both of them. "Is there a problem, ladies?" She asked.

Celine assured her that there was no problem and Avery would prefer privacy. Celine put a pocket knife in the pocket of her dress without them noticing. The man held Avery's hand as they walked away. Avery looked back at Celine with fear in her eyes. Celine mouthed to her that is okay.

At the back of the mansion, Mylan and Sage hid behind a cluster of bushes near the back exit. The night air was crisp, and the tension between them was palpable. Mylan's phone buzzed in his pocket. It was a text from Celine: Avery was called into a private room with a guy.

Mylan's heart skipped a beat as he relayed the message to Sage, keeping his voice low. Sage's reaction was immediate and intense. She demanded they rush in and get Avery out now, fear etched across her face.

Mylan shook his head, trying to calm her down. "If we rush in there right now, they will kill her, Celine, and Warren. We have to play this smart. Avery can handle herself," he said, trying to reassure both himself and Sage.

Sage's frustration was evident. "No, she can't. She damn near had a panic attack when she shot at the guy. This is not going to work," she insisted, her voice tinged with panic.

Mylan placed a hand on her shoulder, urging her to stay quiet and calm down. He reminded her that they needed to stick to the plan and wait for the right moment. The slightest misstep could have catastrophic consequences.

"Are you sure you can trust this girl to cut the phone and wifi service?" he asked, shifting the conversation to their next move. It was crucial for their plan that the communication lines be cut, preventing Veronica and her men from calling for backup.

"Yes," Sage replied, her voice steady despite the turmoil inside her. She pulled out her phone and dialed Tegan.

Tegan was parked in her car on the main road, just close enough to connect to the mansion's network. Her hands moved swiftly over her laptop, tapping into the system with practiced ease. Tegan never asked why they needed her help; she was a ride-or-die for Sage, always ready to step in when it mattered. Besides, she had a knack for hacking and could break into almost any system with minimal effort. She also provided everyone with satellite phones to stay connected once the service was cut.

"I'll cut the service in 5 minutes," Tegan confirmed over the phone, her voice calm and confident. "Once that 5 minutes ends, y'all only have 20 minutes to get in and out before everything goes back up."

"Thank you, Tegan," Sage said, grateful for her friend's unwavering loyalty and skill. "We'll be ready."

After hanging up, Sage sent out a blast text to everyone involved in the operation, alerting them to the time limit. Five minutes to cut the service 30 minutes to get in and out.

Mylan, sensing the gravity of the situation, handed Sage a silencer for her gun. "Here, use this. We can't afford to draw any attention."

Chapter 18

Seconds to Midnight

A guard stepped outside to smoke, his silhouette briefly illuminated by the glow of his lighter. Mylan and Sage stayed hidden, holding their breaths as they watched him take a long drag from his cigarette. This wasn't part of the plan. No one was supposed to be out back, but here he was, disrupting their carefully laid-out scheme.

"60 seconds," Sage whispered to Mylan, counting down the time until Tegan would cut the service. Her heart thudded in her chest; each beat syncing with the countdown in her head.

Mylan glanced at Sage, his eyes narrowing with determination. They couldn't afford to wait any longer. He slowly stood up, his movements silent and calculated. The guard remained oblivious, lost in his thoughts and the haze of smoke.

In a swift motion, Mylan caught the man off guard, raising his silenced gun and pulling the trigger. The shot was muffled, the bullet hitting the guard square in the head. The man's eyes widened briefly in shock before he crumpled to the ground, his cigarette falling beside him, extinguished.

Mylan watched as life left the man's eyes, then quickly signaled for Sage to come forward. They had no time to waste. The service was about to be cut, and they needed to move fast.

The backdoor of Veronica's mansion swung open, revealing a narrow, dimly lit hallway that led deeper into the opulent house. They were far from the main ballroom, but the faint sounds of music and laughter echoed in the distance, a reminder of the party taking place within.

Back inside the bedroom, Avery stood by the door, her heart pounding in her chest. The room was dimly lit, with heavy curtains drawn over the windows, casting shadows across the walls. The man sat on the bed, his eyes fixed on her with a predatory gleam.

"Come here," he ordered, his voice dripping with entitlement. Avery didn't move; her body was tense and rigid as she stood her ground.

"Come sit down," he repeated, his voice rising to a yell. The command echoed through the room, sending a shiver down Avery's spine. Reluctantly, she walked over, each step feeling like a lead weight dragging her forward, and sat on the opposite side of the bed.

The man slid over to Avery, a smug smile on his face as he closed the distance between them. Avery's instincts screamed at her to get away, but she forced herself to stay calm, calculating her next move.

"I'll put on some music," she said, her voice steady as she reached for a nearby speaker, hoping to create a distraction.

He stood up behind her, wrapping his disgusting hands around her waist, his touch sending a wave of revulsion through her. Avery moved away quickly, trying to put some space between them. But he was relentless, grabbing her forearm with a grip like a vice, cursing under his breath.

"Stop playing games," he snarled, pulling her closer, his breath hot and foul against her skin.

He pushed her onto the bed, pinning her beneath his weight. His stomach was huge, pressing down on her like a suffocating blanket, and Avery could barely move. She felt her stomach churn, a wave of nausea rising as fear gripped her.

"You're going to do whatever I tell you to do," he sneered, his face inches from hers.

Avery pleaded with him, her voice trembling, "Please, don't hurt me."

His eyes narrowed, frustration twisting his features. He slapped her across the face, the sharp sting echoing through the room. "Shut up," he snapped, the words filled with menace.

He started to kiss her neck, his breath hot and suffocating. Avery's mind raced as she fought to keep panic at bay. Her fingers brushed against the knife she had hidden in her pocket, the cool metal a lifeline in her desperate situation. She had one chance to get it right.

With a surge of adrenaline, Avery gripped the knife and quickly jammed it into his neck, twisting it with all her strength. The blade pierced his voice box, cutting off his ability to scream.

His eyes widened in shock, his mouth opening in a silent gasp. Blood gushed from the wound, soaking the sheets beneath them. He gurgled, a grotesque sound escaping as he clutched at his throat, his strength ebbing away.

His weight bore down on her, and he collapsed on top of her, dead.

Chapter 19

Close Quarters

Celine paced around the living area where her ladies entertained the men, her eyes scanning the room for any sign of trouble. The atmosphere was thick with laughter, the clinking of glasses, and the low hum of conversation, but her mind was elsewhere. She couldn't shake the worry gnawing at her gut, knowing that Avery was in the private room with one of Veronica's guests.

Celine made her way through the crowd, her heels clicking sharply against the polished marble floors. Her heart raced with each step as she approached Veronica, who stood at the center of a group of admirers. Veronica wore a smile that didn't reach her eyes, her presence as commanding as ever.

Celine cleared her throat, catching Veronica's attention. "I need to check on Avery," Celine said, trying to keep her voice steady. "I want to make sure everything's okay. If anything happens to my girls, we'll have a problem."

Veronica arched an eyebrow, her lips curving into a mocking smile. "Celine, darling, you worry too much. My guests know the rules," she replied, waving a hand dismissively.

Celine's eyes narrowed, her patience wearing thin. "I don't care about your guests, Veronica. I care about my girls. I'm going to see her."

Veronica sighed, a hint of annoyance in her eyes and motioned for one of her men to come over. "Fine, I'll send someone to check. If it puts your mind at ease," she said, her voice dripping with disdain.

She turned to one of her henchmen, a burly man with a no-nonsense demeanor. "Go make sure our guest and the girl are behaving themselves," Veronica ordered, her tone leaving no room for argument.

The man nodded, heading toward the hallway that led to the private rooms. Celine watched him go, a knot of tension in her stomach as she hoped he wouldn't discover anything amiss. She needed this operation to go smoothly for Avery's sake and the success of their plan.

Back inside the bedroom, Avery managed to slide out from under the man's lifeless weight, her heart pounding in her chest. She looked down at her hands, watching them tremble. The room was eerily silent except for her ragged breathing and the faint thrum of music from the party.

She picked up the knife from where it had fallen on the bed and slipped it back into her pocket, the metal still warm from her hand. She needed to move quickly. With every second that passed, the danger of being discovered grew.

Rushing into the bathroom, Avery flicked on the light and caught sight of herself in the mirror. Her reflection stared back at her, face speckled with blood. She felt a wave of nausea roll through her, but she pushed it down, knowing she didn't have the luxury of breaking down.

She quickly turned on the faucet, splashing water over her face to wash away the evidence of what she'd done. The water ran red for a moment before swirling down the drain, leaving her skin clean but her mind still racing.

A crisp white robe hung in the closet beside the sink, the fabric soft and inviting. She pulled it out and wrapped it around herself, hoping it would make her look less conspicuous if someone came in.

Just as she finished tying the robe's belt, a knock echoed from the bedroom door. Avery froze, her heart skipping a beat. Who was it? And, more importantly, what did they want? Fear crept up her spine, but she knew she had to stay calm. She couldn't afford to lose her nerve now.

Taking a deep breath to steady herself, she turned back to the bedroom, her eyes darting to the dead man's body. She grabbed a blanket from the foot of the bed and covered him as best as she could, hoping it would buy her some time. The blood had already begun to seep through, but she prayed it wouldn't be noticed immediately.

Avery cracked the door open just enough to show her face, tilting her head to the side as she forced a smile. She tried to look relaxed and playful, masking the fear and tension bubbling inside. The henchmen's eyes flicked past her to the bed, where the man lay unmoving under the blanket.

"Is he alright?" the guard asked, suspicion lingering in his tone as he studied the scene.

Avery let out a small, light-hearted laugh, trying to sell her story. "Oh, he's just sleeping," she said, her voice laced with a casual nonchalance that contradicted the panic she felt. "I'm about to wake him up for another round. Could you bring us two glasses of champagne?"

He hesitated for a moment, scrutinizing her expression. Avery held her breath, willing him to buy the act. She kept her smile steady, her eyes pleading with him to take her words at face value.

Finally, he nodded, seemingly satisfied with her explanation. "Sure, I'll get those for you," he said, backing away from the door.

Back in the grand hall of Veronica's mansion, the henchman returned to Celine and Veronica's side. He muttered a few words to them, assuring them that Avery was fine and that the situation was under control. Veronica nodded with a slight smirk, satisfied with his report. He then moved toward the bar to grab two glasses of champagne for the "sleeping" guest and his young companion.

Avery stood by the door, listening to the soft click as it closed behind the henchman. Her heart raced, but she forced herself to remain calm. The henchman walked past her, his mind already on the champagne flutes in his hand as he approached the table.

As he turned his back to her, she saw her chance. Avery's hand slipped into her pocket, fingers curling around the handle of the knife. With one swift motion, she drew it out and plunged it into his back with all her strength, the blade slicing through fabric and flesh.

He gasped; a strangled noise escaped his lips, but she didn't hesitate. She pulled the knife out and struck again. He never got a chance to fight back and crumpled to the ground, lifeless, leaving Avery standing there, her breath coming in ragged gasps.

Her heart was pounding so loudly that it echoed in her ears. She glanced down at her hands, sticky with blood, and then at the discarded robe she had worn to cover her blood-stained clothes. It was time to move.

Chapter 20

Blood Ties

$\mathbf{M}$ ylan and Sage moved cautiously down the dimly lit hallway, their footsteps barely making a sound on the plush carpet. The walls were lined with ornate sconces, casting flickering shadows that danced eerily as they progressed deeper into the mansion's maze-like interior.

As they neared the end of the hallway, the low murmur of voices reached their ears. Two men were engaged in a conversation, their tones casual yet carrying the unmistakable air of authority. From the snippets they could hear, Mylan and Sage quickly realized these were Veronica's henchmen.

Sage glanced at Mylan, her eyes wide with apprehension. She waited for his cue, knowing their next move was crucial. Mylan met her gaze, his expression calm and focused. He put his finger over his lips, signaling for her to remain silent and follow his lead.

Sage stood behind Mylan, her breath steady but heart racing as they waited for the two men to walk past. The dimly lit corridor seemed to close in around them, the tension thick in the air. Mylan held his gun at the ready, eyes fixed on the approaching figures.

As the first henchman walked past, Mylan swiftly stepped out, pressing the barrel of his gun against the man's head. The henchman froze, his eyes widening in surprise.

"Be quiet and don't make a sound," Mylan demanded, his voice low and commanding.

The henchman sneered, a cocky grin spreading across his face. "You know who you're fucking with?"

Sage moved from behind Mylan, her own gun held steady in her hands. "Naw, but you about to find out," she said, her voice laced with confidence.

The second henchman caught off guard, raised his hands slowly. The two men exchanged glances, their bravado quickly giving way to caution as they realized the situation had turned against them.

Mylan gestured with his gun, indicating that the men should move against the wall. "Hands where I can see them," he ordered.

Sage stood beside him, keeping her weapon trained on the men as they obeyed. She watched as they dropped their earpieces and guns to the ground. Mylan nodded in satisfaction, then glanced at Sage.

She understood his unspoken cue and stepped forward, eyes narrowing as she focused on the man closest to her. "Where's Warren?" she asked, her voice calm but insistent.

Both men ignored Sage, their defiance only fueling her rage. Without missing a beat, she swung the butt of her gun at the nearest henchman, striking him over the head with a resounding thud. Blood quickly seeped from the wound, dripping down his face as he stumbled back, a pained grimace twisting his features.

"He's downstairs. Damn," the henchman groaned, clutching his bloody head, the pain clearly making him more compliant.

The other man smirked, his eyes cold and taunting as he turned to Mylan. "You're not getting out of here alive. Just like your wife," he sneered, relishing the words like a twisted victory.

Mylan's face darkened, a flash of anger passing over his features. Without hesitation, he pulled the trigger, and the henchman crumpled to the ground, lifeless.

Mylan kneeled down in front of the remaining henchman, who looked at his dead partner with wide, terrified eyes. "You see him?" Mylan asked, his voice dangerously calm as he pointed to the corpse sprawled on the floor. "That's going to be you if you don't tell me exactly how to get downstairs."

The henchman's voice quivered as he explained the layout of the mansion. "Behind the bookshelf in the library, there's a hidden panel. It leads to the basement," he stammered, his eyes darting between Mylan and Sage. "The room you're looking for is the first door on the right."

He looked desperately at Mylan, his fear palpable. "Please, I told you everything. Don't kill me," he pleaded his voice barely a whisper.

Mylan, however, showed no mercy. With a cold, steady hand, he raised his gun and pulled the trigger, and the man slumped lifelessly to the floor.

Chapter 21

Smoke and Mirrors

Celine stood beside Veronica in the main room of the mansion. The air was thick with cigarette smoke, the low hum of conversation mingling with the clinking of glasses. The mood was relaxed yet charged, with a palpable undercurrent of danger.

Celine glanced down at her phone, noting the time. They only had 15 minutes to get Warren out. As the night wore on, Veronica's demeanor shifted from amused to increasingly tense, a sign that something was amiss. Her icy gaze scanned the room, watching her guests with the calculating eyes of a predator.

A henchman approached Veronica, leaning in to whisper something in her ear. Veronica's expression darkened, her suspicion clearly piqued.

"Everything okay?" Celine asked, feigning nonchalance as she took a sip from her drink.

Veronica ignored her question, stepping to the side with her henchman to discuss the issue privately. Her body language was tense, a clear indication that she was on high alert.

Realizing that their carefully laid plans were in jeopardy, Celine discreetly sent a text to the team: "Veronica knows something is up. We need a distraction NOW. Get Avery and Warren out safely."

Nora and Luke stood just outside the edge of the trees, their voices hushed but tense as they continued to argue. The night air was cool against their skin, and the distant sound of the party filtered through the trees, a stark contrast to the urgent conversation unfolding between them.

"It almost feels like you're arguing just to distract me from what we need to do," Nora snapped, her frustration boiling over. "Time is running out, and I don't want to hear this shit."

Her phone vibrated, interrupting her thoughts. She glanced at the screen, reading Celine's text: "Veronica knows something is happening. We need a distraction."

Nora knew they had to act fast, but her options were limited. The only other thing she had on her besides her gun was a grenade. She looked at Luke, her mind racing. Should she throw it?

"You can't throw that," Luke warned, his eyes widening with urgency. "Our people are inside."

But Nora's instincts told her they needed to create a diversion, something big enough to pull all eyes away from the mission. She pulled the pin and hurled the grenade toward the mansion, aiming for the patch of grass near the front of the house.

The explosion ripped through the night with a deafening roar, the sound like a thunderclap that shattered the stillness. A plume of smoke and debris erupted into the air, the shockwave sending a powerful blast that knocked Nora and Luke off their feet.

Inside the mansion, the explosion sent a shockwave of panic through the room. The girls scattered to one side, their faces masks of fear and confusion, while the men hurriedly gathered their belongings, some with the air of men who knew they were in deep trouble if caught here.

Veronica's face darkened with fury. Her icy demeanor cracked for just a moment, revealing the anger bubbling beneath. "What the hell was that?" she barked, her voice cutting through the chaos like a knife. "Find out what's going on!"

She motioned sharply to her henchmen, who sprang into action, weapons at the ready as they moved to investigate the source of the explosion.

Veronica shot Celine a cold glance. "Get your girls and pack up your things," she ordered, her voice dripping with authority. "This party is over."

As Veronica strode away, her heels clicking sharply against the marble floor. Once she was sure Veronica was out of sight, she turned to her girls, her voice low but urgent. "Get your shit together and get out of here now," she said, waving them towards the door.

With the chaos from the explosion still reverberating through the mansion, Celine knew they had a small window to make their move. She raced down the hallway, her heart pounding with adrenaline and fear for Avery.

When Celine reached the door to the room where she'd last seen Avery, she paused for a moment, preparing herself for whatever she might find inside. She pushed the door open, and her breath caught in her throat at the sight before her.

The room was a scene straight out of a horror movie. Blood stained the cream-colored carpet and splattered across the walls in chaotic patterns that seemed to mock the elegant decor. The body of the man Avery had stabbed lay slumped on the bed, the sheets soaked in dark crimson, and the henchmen lay dead on the floor.

Avery stood frozen, the bloody knife still clutched tightly in her hand, her breath coming in quick, shallow bursts. Celine stepped into the room, her eyes quickly assessing the situation. Without wasting a moment, she grabbed Avery's arm and pulled her toward the door. "We can't go out the front," she whispered urgently as they slipped into the dimly lit hallway.

The air was thick with tension as they navigated the narrow corridor. They could hear the muffled sounds of chaos from the party—people shouting, Veronica's men barking orders, footsteps echoing through the halls.

"We need to find another way out," Celine said, her voice barely audible over the pounding of their hearts.

As they turned a corner, the sound of approaching footsteps made them freeze. Celine's instincts kicked in; she pulled out her gun, and Avery, still holding the knife, braced herself for whatever lay ahead.

Just then, Mylan and Sage came around the corner. Celine and Avery took a deep breath, relief washing over their tense expressions. Sage tucked her gun back into her waistband as she stared at Avery's bloody clothes.

"What the fuck happened?" she asked, pulling Avery into a tight hug to assure her that everything would be okay.

Mylan quickly explained to Celine and Avery where Warren was being held. "We gotta hurry up because if we get caught on these cameras, we're fucked," he warned, glancing nervously around the dimly lit hallway.

A cold, mocking voice echoed from down the hall, chilling them to the bone. "You're already fucked."

They all turned in unison, their eyes widening as Veronica emerged from the shadows, flanked by four of her henchmen. She wore a triumphant smile, her eyes glimmering with malice.

Mylan quickly pushed Sage and Avery behind him, his mind racing. He knew they were outnumbered and needed a way to turn the tables. Reaching into his pocket, he grabbed a smoke bomb and tossed it toward Veronica and her men.

The bomb exploded with a loud bang, filling the hallway with a cloud of thick, blinding smoke that swirled around them like a living entity. It caught everyone off guard, including Celine, Sage, and Avery.

"Run!" Mylan screamed, his voice barely audible over the confusion.

Sage and Avery sprinted down the dimly lit corridor, the sound of their footsteps echoing off the polished wooden floors. They were frantically searching for the library, knowing that's where Warren was being held.

Finally, they found it. The library loomed before them, a grand and imposing room filled with towering bookshelves that stretched up to the ornate ceiling. Dust motes danced in the air, caught in the dim glow of a single overhead chandelier. The scent of old leather and musty paper hung thick, adding to the room's sense of antiquity.

"The door is behind the bookshelf," Sage said, her voice barely above a whisper, urgency cutting through her words.

Before they could move, a hand shot out from the shadows, grabbing Avery from behind. She screamed, panic flooding her senses as one of Veronica's henchmen yanked her back, his grip like iron around her throat.

Desperation gave Avery a surge of strength. Her hand shot to the knife she'd kept hidden, and with a quick motion, she jammed it into the henchman's arm. The blade sank in, and he howled in pain, his grip loosening just enough for Avery to wrench herself free.

The man staggered back, clutching his wounded arm, blood seeping through his fingers. Sage seized the moment. Her hands were steady as she aimed her gun and squeezed the trigger. The sound of the shot echoed through the library, and the man staggered backward, clutching his chest before collapsing to the floor.

Sage rushed to Avery's side, pulling her up with a firm grip. "Come on, we have to move," she urged.

Avery's hands trembled as she pulled the book, and the bookshelf finally swung open with a low creak, revealing a hidden passage. They exchanged a quick, determined glance, knowing that time was slipping away. Only five minutes remained before the security cameras would come back online, and they couldn't afford to get caught, especially by Veronica, who would relish the chance to turn them over to the police for breaking and entering.

Before them, a narrow staircase descended into darkness, leading to the secret room where Warren was likely being held. Sage and Avery moved quickly, their footsteps echoing off the stone walls as they hurried down the steps. The air grew cooler and more oppressive the deeper they went, the shadows thickening around them.

As they reached the bottom of the staircase, they faced another door, solid and unyielding. Sage's heart pounded in her chest as she pressed her ear against it, straining to hear any sounds from within.

"Warren?" Sage called out; her voice filled with desperation.

There was a brief moment of silence, and then a shuffling sound came from the other side. Sage's heart leaped as she heard a familiar voice.

"Sage? Is that you?" Warren's voice was muffled but unmistakable.

Sage's heart skipped a beat when she heard Warren's voice from inside the room. Relief washed over her, but the urgency of the situation kept her focused. She quickly assessed the door, noticing the lock was the only barrier between them and Warren.

Avery pointed to the lock, her eyes wide with determination. "There," she said, her voice steady.

Sage nodded, her mind racing. "Warren, move back from the door!" she called out, raising her gun.

There was a moment of hesitation from inside, followed by the sound of Warren shuffling away. Sage took a deep breath and fired at the lock, the loud crack of the gunshot echoing in the confined space. The lock shattered, pieces falling to the ground with a metallic clatter.

Together, Sage and Avery used all their strength to pull the heavy door open, their muscles straining as it finally gave way.

Warren stood in the dimly lit room, looking disheveled and worn. His clothes were rumpled, his hair unkempt, and a cloth wrapped around one of his fingers was stained with dried blood. The sight of him was both a relief and a heartache, a testament to the ordeal he had endured.

Sage's eyes filled with tears as she took in his appearance. She rushed forward, throwing her arms around him in a tight embrace. Warren was momentarily caught off guard, his body tensing before he relaxed into her hug.

"We don't have time. Let's go!" Avery urged, her voice cutting through the haze of panic.

Sage, Warren, and Avery sprinted up the narrow staircase, their footsteps pounding against the stone as they raced against the clock. Every second felt like an eternity, the chaos above echoing down the passageway like a living thing. Warren followed closely behind, his breath coming in ragged gasps as they emerged into the mayhem of the mansion.

Sage led the way, her mind laser-focused on getting them out. They dodged past a hail of bullets that ricocheted off walls and shattered glass. Sage eyes scanned for the quickest path to the back exit. Avery stayed close, her heart racing as she tried to keep up with Sage's determined pace.

Just as they reached the hallway leading to freedom, Avery came to a halt. Her mind flashed back to the family still inside. "What about Uncle Mylan and Celine?" she asked, her voice tinged with worry.

Sage hesitated, glancing back at the chaos unfolding behind them. Her heart ached with the weight of her responsibility, torn between the need to save Warren and the loyalty she felt to Mylan and Celine. But she knew they had a plan, and every second counted.

"They'll be okay," Sage assured Avery, her voice firm with conviction. "We have to trust them to handle it." She gently but firmly pulled Avery by the arm, steering her toward the open door that beckoned like a lifeline.

Chapter 22

The Fallout

Outside the mansion, Nora and Luke stood amidst the chaos, their guns still warm from the shootout with Veronica's henchmen. The air was thick with the scent of gunpowder and the echoes of the gunfire that had only just subsided. Tension hung heavy in the night, but there was no time to dwell on it.

Sage, Avery, and Warren appeared through the haze, running toward them with urgency in their steps. Nora's heart skipped a beat as she saw them, relief washing over her like a wave. She rushed forward, pulling Sage and Avery into a tight embrace, holding them close as if to shield them from all the dangers of the world.

"Thank God you're safe," Nora whispered, her voice choked with emotion as she released them from her grip. Her eyes scanned over them, checking for injuries, the weight of the night's events etched on her face.

But then her gaze shifted, and she noticed the absence of her brother and friend. The relief that had momentarily washed over her was replaced with dread. Her eyes locked onto Sage's, searching for answers. "Where's Mylan and Celine?" she asked, her voice laced with worry.

"They're still inside," Sage said, her voice tinged with urgency as she glanced back at the mansion.

A car came speeding down the large driveway, tires screeching as it came to a sudden halt in front of them. The door swung open, and Tegan leaned out, her expression a mix of determination and anxiety. "Come on, now," she warned, waving them over.

The sense of urgency in her voice was clear, and the group quickly moved to the car.

Everyone piled into the car, hearts pounding, except for Nora. She stood firm, her eyes fixed on the mansion as if willing Mylan and Celine to appear.

"I'm not leaving here without my brother and Celine," Nora said, her voice resolute and unwavering. She looked at the others, then back at the mansion, the weight of her words hanging heavily in the air.

Tegan hesitated, her hands gripping the steering wheel as she looked between Nora and the road ahead. Every instinct told her to drive away, to get them to safety, but she understood the loyalty that kept Nora rooted to the spot.

"Mom, please—" Avery began, but Sage placed a hand on her shoulder, understanding the impossible choice her mother faced.

Luke stepped up beside Nora, a fierce look of determination in his eyes. "I'm staying too," he said, leaving no room for argument. "We'll bring them back."

A tense silence filled the air as the group weighed their options. Tegan looked back at Sage, who gave her a small nod of understanding.

"Alright," Tegan finally said, her voice barely above a whisper. She knew the stakes, knew what they were risking, but Sage's nod was all the assurance she needed. She threw the car into gear and pulled away, the tires kicking up gravel as they sped down the driveway.

Inside the car, Avery looked back, watching her mother and Luke grow smaller in the distance. Her heart ached with worry, but she trusted that Nora knew what she was doing.

The cameras were back on, their red lights blinking as if warning them of the danger. Still, Nora and Luke rushed inside the mansion, driven by a strong need to find Mylan and Celine. The gunfire had stopped, leaving behind a heavy silence that felt strange and unsettling. The once beautiful mansion was now a war zone, showing signs of chaos and destruction.

Smoke lingered in the air, curling around the furniture and drifting through the halls like a ghostly mist. The smoke bomb had turned the grand mansion into a confusing maze of shadows and debris.

Nora and Luke moved carefully, their footsteps echoing on the marble floors. Every corner they turned revealed more destruction, broken glass, and overturned furniture. It was clear that a fierce battle had happened just moments before.

"Mylan! Celine!" Nora called out, her voice steady but full of urgency. Her eyes scanned the room, looking for any sign of them in the wreckage.

Luke stayed close, his senses on high alert as he looked around. "They've got to be here somewhere," he said, trying to reassure himself.

The mansion felt different now. The grand look and feel were overshadowed by the tension in the air. Each shadow seemed to move, and every creak of the floorboards sent chills down their spines.

Nora stopped, listening carefully for any sound that might lead them to Mylan and Celine. The silence was heavy, making it hard to breathe.

They stumbled upon Mylan and Celine, who were taking cover behind an overturned table. Celine was crouched over Mylan, pressing her hands against his arm where blood seeped through his shirt. His face was pale, but his eyes were focused and alert.

Nora rushed over, her heart pounding in her chest. "Mylan, are you okay?" she asked, her voice thick with concern.

Celine nodded, her expression tense but determined. "He's fine, but we need to get out of here before Veronica and her men come back," she said, glancing nervously down the dimly lit corridor.

Nora helped Mylan to his feet, supporting his weight as he steadied himself. But as she did, something shifted inside her—a mix of fear and anger, a burning need for justice. Her eyes blazed with fury.

"There's just one more thing I need to do," she said, her voice cold.

As Mylan, Celine, and Luke headed for the exit, keeping a watchful eye on the mansion's darkened halls, Nora lingered behind. She reached for the mini gas can bottle hooked to her jeans, feeling the cool metal against her skin.

She unscrewed the cap and began pouring the gas along the hallway floor, the strong smell rising sharply in the air. The liquid spread in a slick trail, glistening under the flickering lights as if eager to ignite.

Suddenly, she heard footsteps; a rapid, thunderous march of boots echoed off the walls. Her heart leaped in her chest as she looked up to see Veronica and her henchmen rounding the corner.

Veronica's eyes locked onto Nora, a smirk playing at the corners of her mouth. "Going somewhere?" she taunted, her voice dripped with venom.

The henchmen behind her were like a wall of muscle, their expressions hard and ready for a fight. They moved with confidence, closing the distance between them and Nora with each determined step.

Nora's mind raced, calculating her next move. Her fingers trembled as she reached for the lighter in her pocket, the weight of it both comforting and terrifying. She could feel the heat of their approach, the danger they represented looming like a storm cloud.

But there was no turning back. Not now. Not when her family was at stake.

Nora didn't waste any time. She flicked her lighter open, and the hallway went up in flames, the fire spreading rapidly across the floor. The intense heat and crackling sound filled the air, consuming everything in its path. She watched for a split second as the flames roared to life, casting a fierce glow that painted the walls in a hellish orange.

"You messed with the wrong bitch," Nora muttered under her breath, adrenaline surging through her veins. She turned and sprinted towards the back door, her footsteps echoing behind her.

As she burst through the door, Nora could hear Veronica's furious shouts and the chaos erupting inside. The henchmen scrambled, caught off guard by the sudden blaze as the smell of burning wood and smoke filled the air.

Outside, Mylan, Celine, and Luke were already waiting, their eyes wide with urgency. Nora joined them, and together, they ran, their feet pounding against the earth as they made their escape.

Chapter 23

Silent Confessions

Back at Mylan's condo, the atmosphere was thick with tension and unease. The soft glow of a single lamp cast long shadows on the walls. The faint hum of the city outside was barely audible, a distant reminder of the ordinary world they were momentarily detached from.

Sage, Avery, Tegan, and Warren were gathered in the living room, the air buzzing with anxious energy. Each of them carried the weight of the night's events, their minds racing with thoughts of what had just happened and what might come next.

Sage leaned against the wall, her arms crossed, her eyes fixed on Tegan. "Tegan, you don't have to stay. I've already got you into some shit you shouldn't be in," she said.

Tegan sat comfortably on the couch, a small smile playing on her lips. She waved a dismissive hand, her eyes sparkling with excitement. "Well, I already told my parents I was sleeping over, so that's a negative," she replied, leaning back against the cushions. "And plus, this is so exciting. I've never had this much fun in my life."

Warren, sitting nearby with a bandage wrapped around his injured finger, watched Tegan with a knowing look. He shook his head, a faint smile tugging at the corners of his lips. "You've never been in a fight, have you?" he said, his tone not questioning but stating the obvious.

Tegan chuckled, brushing off his comment with a shrug. "What gave it away?" she joked, trying to lighten the mood.

But Warren's eyes were serious, reflecting the gravity of their situation. "It's not all fun and games, you know," he said, his voice carrying a weight of experience and caution.

The cool night air enveloped them as Sage and Warren stepped out onto the balcony, leaving the tense atmosphere of the living room behind. The city stretched out below them, a wide spread of twinkling lights and distant sounds.

Warren leaned against the railing, his eyes reflecting gratitude. "Thank you," he spoke first, his voice carrying a sincerity that cut through the silence.

Sage, standing beside him, turned to meet his gaze. "You would have done the same for me. I hope," she replied, a faint smile tugging at her lips.

Warren's expression softened, his eyes showing a depth of emotion that spoke volumes. "I would do anything for you and more," he said, his words laced with a quiet intensity.

Sage held his gaze, and for a moment, there was something inside her that believed him, a flicker of trust she hadn't felt with him before. She took a deep breath, feeling the weight of the night pressing against her chest.

"I'm in a substance abuse treatment program for cocaine use," Sage admitted, her voice barely above a whisper.

"Because of me and what I made you do, I am deeply sorry," Warren said, his voice heavy with regret. "That's not the person I am, and that's not even the person I was. I was hurt by your mother, and I wanted to hurt her the same way. If I knew that you were my daughter... I would—"

Sage gently interrupted him by raising a respectful hand, signaling him to stop. "When I started the program, I blamed you," she admitted, her voice steady but filled with emotion. "But to tell you the truth, there was some part of me that didn't want to be here."

Warren's brow furrowed. "What do you mean by that?" he asked, his voice soft, as if afraid of the answer.

Sage took a deep breath. "After my father Henry died, and I found out he wasn't my real father, I felt lost. Like my whole life was a lie," she confessed, her words cutting through the quiet night air. "I wanted to die. I didn't see the point of being here anymore."

The city lights flickered like distant stars as Sage and Warren stood together on the balcony, the night air filled with unspoken truths. Warren hesitated, his eyes clouded with regret and pain.

"I killed Henry because there was still a part of me that is still in love with Nora," he confessed, his voice barely above a whisper. "I hated the fact that she moved on and forgot about me and didn't tell me that you were my child. What I did was wrong, and I will always carry the guilt that I took your father away."

Warren's words hung heavily in the air, a confession that revealed the raw wound of his actions. He looked at Sage, his eyes pleading for understanding, for forgiveness.

Sage's eyes filled with tears as she met his gaze. She felt a storm of emotions churning inside her; anger, sadness, and longing. She looked down, trying to find the right words, trying to make sense of the chaos in her heart.

The truth was, she had spent so long hating him, blaming him for the loss and confusion that had shattered her life. But now, standing before him, she saw a man tormented by his own demons, a man seeking redemption.

"I know," Sage said softly, her voice trembling with emotion. Her eyes met his, a silent understanding passing between them. "But I don't want to hate you."

Sage took a soft breath, the air catching in her throat as she searched for the strength to say what she truly felt. "I just want you to be my dad," she admitted, her voice breaking but firm.

The words were a lifeline, a bridge reaching across the chasm that had separated them for so long. It was a chance for healing, for rebuilding what had been lost.

Warren's eyes glistened with unshed tears, his heart aching at the vulnerability and strength in his daughter's words. He reached out, gently placing a hand on her shoulder, a tentative step toward the connection he had longed for.

"I want that too, Sage," he said, his voice filled with sincerity and hope. "I want to be there for you, to make things right. It won't be easy, but I promise I'll try my best."

"Hey," a familiar voice said gently, trying not to intrude on the moment.

Warren and Sage turned to find Nora standing in the doorway, her presence a warm and comforting force. Sage's heart swelled with emotion, and she quickly ran to her mother.

"Mom," Sage whispered, wrapping her arms around Nora in a tight embrace. Nora hugged her back, her touch tender and reassuring.

As Nora held Sage, she looked over at Warren. Their eyes met, a silent exchange passing between them. Warren's face showed relief and uncertainty, hoping that Nora hadn't overheard the raw confession he had shared with Sage.

Nora gave him a nod, a silent acknowledgment of the complexity and pain that lay beneath the surface. Despite everything, they were a family bound by blood and the desire to heal the wounds of the past.

After a moment, Sage pulled away, and Nora offered her a reassuring smile before turning to greet the others. She walked over to Mylan, Celine, and Luke, who stood waiting nearby.

Nora stepped out onto the balcony, the sliding door clicking shut behind her. The cool night air brushed against her skin, but it did little to calm the turmoil inside. She found Warren standing there, his gaze lost in the distance.

"You still love me?" she asked, her voice carried the weight of years of unspoken feelings. Her appearance was full of vulnerability, but her eyes held a glimmer of determination.

Warren stiffened, his shoulders tensing as he heard her words. He didn't turn to face her, keeping his eyes fixed on the horizon. "You weren't supposed to hear all of that," he admitted, a hint of regret lacing his tone.

"Well, I did," Nora replied, stepping closer to him, her eyes searching for answers in the silence that hung between them. "Tell me."

Warren's expression hardened, and his eyes narrowed. "What does it matter? You're engaged," he said, his voice edged with bitterness.

Nora felt a pang in her chest, the truth of his words cutting deeper than she expected. She took a step closer, her eyes searching his face for any sign of the man she had once known so well. "When I made you take the fall...did you love me?" she asked, her voice soft but insistent.

Warren turned to face her fully, his eyes reflecting a turbulent of emotions. The weight of their shared past hung between them like an unspoken confession. "I'm in love with you now," he admitted, his voice cracking with sincerity. He swallowed hard, the admission bringing a vulnerability he had tried to conceal.

Chapter 24

The Last Stand

Nora felt a lump form in her stomach as Warren's words echoed in her mind. After everything that had happened between them, all the betrayals and lies, he still loved her. It was a truth she hadn't been prepared to face.

"You should have told me," Nora said, her voice barely above a whisper. "Why didn't you tell me?"

Warren's eyes flashed with frustration and longing, emotions he had kept buried for too long. "What the hell does it matter, Nora?" he replied, his voice filled with anger and pain. "You've made your choices. We're on different paths now."

Nora opened her mouth to respond, the words hanging on the tip of her tongue. "Because I—"

Before she could finish, the sliding door burst open, breaking the fragile tension between them. Nora turned to see Luke standing there, urgency written across his face.

"The casino's alarm system was triggered," Luke announced, his voice cutting through the night air like a cold wind.

The conversation was abruptly cut short as Nora and Warren hurried back inside. The tension in the air was palpable, and there was a shared understanding that Veronica might be making a move against them.

The group exchanged worried glances, the gravity of the situation settling in. The realization that Veronica's reach was far and wide set a sense of urgency among them.

"We need to get to the casino," Luke said, his voice firm.

Mylan nodded in agreement, the seriousness of the threat mirrored in his eyes. "If Veronica's making her move, we can't afford to sit back and wait."

Nora looked at each of them, feeling the weight of their collective responsibility. "Warren, are you up for this?" she asked, knowing he was still recovering but trusting his instincts.

Warren gave a determined nod, his face a mask of resolve. "I'm in. We need to end this."

Celine, who had been observing the conversation with a keen eye, stepped forward. "I'll stay behind and keep an eye on the girls," she offered her voice steady but with a hint of concern. "You all go. Make sure this ends tonight."

Sage and Avery exchanged a glance, understanding the seriousness of the situation. "Be careful, Mom," Sage said, her voice tinged with both worry and trust. "And dad."

Nora gave her daughters a reassuring look, her heart heavy with the responsibility she carried. "We'll be back soon," she promised, her voice steady despite the storm of emotions within.

The night air was heavy with tension as Nora, Warren, Mylan, and Luke approached the casino. They moved cautiously, their senses heightened, each step bringing them closer to a potential showdown with Veronica.

Once inside, the dim lights and the low hum of the slot machines set an eerie atmosphere. The casino, usually bustling with activity, felt different, charged with an undercurrent of impending danger.

Veronica sat at a slot machine, her henchmen flanking her like a pack of wolves. Her presence was commanding, her demeanor icy. She exuded a calm confidence, but her eyes burned with vengeance, a clear signal that she was ready for whatever was about to unfold.

The sound of coins clinking from the slot machine was the only noise cutting through the silence as Nora and her group entered the room. Guns drawn, they moved with precision, each aware of the gravity of the situation.

Veronica spun around in her seat, her feet stopping her abruptly as she faced them. A smirk played on her lips, a chilling difference from the fierce intensity in her eyes.

"Well, well, well," she said, her voice dripping with disdain. "The troops have landed... I can't believe you thought you could come to my home fuck it up and then take off into the sunset."

"We are not doing this with you, V," Luke said, his voice steady but laced with underlying tension, gun still pointed directly at her.

Veronica's eyes flared with anger, her composure slipping. "You don't call me V. You lost the right to call me that," she yelled, her voice echoing in the spacious room.

Nora glanced at Luke with furrowed brows. The way he casually addressed Veronica didn't sit right with her. Why did he call her V? What did it mean? The questions swirled in her mind, unsettling her in a way she hadn't anticipated.

Her eyes flicked between Veronica and Luke, searching for clues for any indication of a deeper connection that she hadn't been aware of. A shadow of doubt crept into her thoughts, unsettling her focus.

Veronica rose from her seat with an unyielding grace that made her intentions unmistakably clear. Her henchmen, as if responding to an unspoken command, moved in perfect unison, their eyes fixed on the targets before them. Mylan,

Nora, Warren, and Luke stepped back, feeling the weight of what was coming.

"This back and forth has gotten boring," Veronica declared, her voice cold and dismissive. "I am no longer asking for the casino back. I am taking it." Her gaze swept over them like a predator surveying its prey. "As for my deceased husband and son, You know I can't allow you to continue to breathe."

Her words were a death sentence, hanging in the air like a heavy fog. With a snap of her fingers, her henchmen moved into position, ready to attack. It was a terrifying moment, the calm before the storm, where everyone knew things were about to explode.

Just as she turned away, ready to let her henchmen do their work, Veronica paused. The room was silent, waiting for her next move.

"One more thing... Mylan," she said, turning back with a sly grin. "I didn't order the hit on Sarah." She winked at him, adding, "Just thought you should know."

Mylan was stunned. Everything that happened that night was because of Sarah's death. If Veronica wasn't behind it, then who was? He looked around the casino, the gaudy lights flickering overhead, and noticed that Luke had disappeared. "Son of a bitch," Mylan muttered under his breath, feeling a cold dread settle in his stomach like ice water.

Nora and Warren realized Luke was gone, too. Confusion etched across their faces mirrored Mylan's own.

Veronica turned to leave, her heels digging into the plush carpet with a sense of cold triumph. But before she could take another step, a gunshot cracked through the air, and her body collapsed to the ground with a sickening thud. Her eyes widened with shock for a fleeting moment before the light faded from them completely.

The suddenness of the shot caught everyone off guard. Her henchmen, initially frozen in place, scrambled for cover, realizing someone was shooting from the office on the second floor. From there, they had a perfect vantage point overlooking the chaotic ground floor below.

Warren and Mylan seized the moment. With adrenaline coursing through their veins like fire, they charged forward, engaging the disoriented henchmen. The air was filled with the deafening sound of gunfire, echoing off the walls of the grand casino hall.

Warren moved with swift precision, each shot carefully aimed. His face was a mask of determination, a man on a mission to protect his family and finally put an end to Veronica's terror. His heart pounded like a war drum, but his hands were steady and sure.

Mylan fought alongside him, his mind a whirlwind of emotions, but he was a man avenging not only his wife's death but also reclaiming his family's safety. Each shot fired was a step closer to justice, and he moved with a fury that made him unstoppable.

Amidst the mayhem, Nora lingered behind. She needed to find Luke, confront him, and discover where his true loyalties lay. Her instincts told her he was hiding something, and she wasn't about to let him get away with it.

Nora's heart skipped a beat as Luke emerged from behind a slot machine, a smirk curling his lips. The dim casino lights cast shadows across his face, revealing a sinister satisfaction in his eyes. Nora felt a chill run through her, and her brows knitted, and her mouth opened slightly in disbelief.

"You had Sarah killed? Why?" Nora's voice quivered, a storm of shock and anger tightening her throat.

Luke laughed, a sound that seemed to fill the room with its coldness. "The only thing stopping me from living comfortably and owning this casino was Veronica. I knew once I killed Harry, she would come after me." He leaned against the slot machine, his eyes glinting with a twisted satisfaction.

Nora felt her stomach churn at his words. Her hands clenched into fists at her sides, her nails digging into her palms as she tried to steady herself. Her heart pounded in her chest, each beat echoing with the realization of Luke's betrayal.

"The fact that Sage took out Que was the icing on the cake. I knew she wouldn't let that go," Luke continued, his voice dripping with smugness.

"You played me," Nora said, her voice sharp with anger, her words slicing through the tension like a knife. Her hands were trembling, but she clenched them into fists, trying to maintain control.

Luke tilted his head, a smug grin on his face as he reveled in her fury. "I needed you to get rid of Veronica so I didn't have to deal with her, and when you wanted to sign over the papers." He shook his head, chuckling softly. "I couldn't have that."

Nora's eyes widened, and her heart felt heavy, like a weight pressing down on her chest. "So you had Sarah killed because you knew Mylan would want vengeance." Her voice was steady, but there was an undercurrent of hurt that she couldn't hide.

Luke's grin widened as if he took pleasure in confirming her suspicions. "You're so smart," he taunted, his eyes shining with twisted amusement.

Nora's jaw clenched as she fought back tears, refusing to let them fall. She took a deep breath, steadying herself before meeting his gaze.

"Now what? Veronica is dead. Now what?" she asked, her voice low and fierce, each word laced with the weight of her emotions. She took a step closer, her eyes locked on his, daring him to reveal his next move.

On the other side of the casino, Douglas, Warren, and Mylan stood amidst the aftermath, surrounded by the lifeless bodies of Veronica's henchmen. The air was thick with the smell of gunpowder, and the silence that followed the chaos was deafening.

Douglas wiped the sweat from his brow, his eyes scanning the room for any remaining threats. He was breathing heavily, the adrenaline from the shootout still coursing through his veins. Warren leaned against a slot machine, his body slumping with relief, while Mylan checked his arm, still bandaged from the earlier bullet wound.

Mylan glanced up, catching Douglas's eye. "How did you know we were here?" he asked.

Douglas grinned, a hint of satisfaction in his eyes. "Sage called and said that you needed backup," he replied, his tone casual. "And once I threatened Captain Langford about his connection to Veronica, let's just say he came around."

Warren chuckled, shaking his head in disbelief. "I'm just glad this is over with."

Douglas nodded, his smile widening as the tension in the room began to dissipate. "My people are coming in now," he added.

The three men exchanged a look, a silent acknowledgment of the battle they had just fought and won. For a moment, it seemed as though the nightmare was finally over, and a sense of relief washed over them.

But just as they began to relax, a single gunshot rang out, cutting through the air like a knife.

Warren, Mylan, and Douglas sprinted toward the sound of the gunshot, their hearts pounding in their chests. As they rounded a corner, they came to a sudden halt, horror-struck by the sight that greeted them.

Nora lay on the casino floor, a pool of crimson spreading beneath her as a gunshot wound marred her chest. Her eyes fluttered, trying to focus as she gasped for breath. The bright casino lights above cast a harsh glow on her pale face, highlighting the stark reality of her injury.

Douglas's hands flew to his face, covering it as he spun away from the scene, unable to bear the sight of Nora, "Fuck," he muttered, the word escaping him like a pained whisper, the weight of the situation crashing down on him.

Mylan stood frozen, his body tense and his fists clenched at his sides. His gaze was fixed on Nora, yet he couldn't bring himself to step closer, as if moving forward would make the scene all too real. "Where is he?" Mylan shouted, his voice raw with fury and desperation. "I'm going to kill him!" He simmered, avoiding looking directly at Nora, his rage directed outward to Luke, who was nowhere to be seen.

Warren fell to his knees beside Nora, his face a mask of agony as tears streamed down uncontrollably. He gathered Nora into his arms, cradling her as if he could somehow shield her from the pain.

"Be...cause I..." Nora gasped, each word a struggle as blood bubbled at the corners of her mouth. Her eyes, once filled with fire, now seemed distant, but she fought to keep them on Warren. "Love... you."

With those final words, her body went limp, life slipping away from her like sand through his fingers.

"Nora, no! Please don't do this to me!" Warren's voice broke, raw and guttural, a sound of pure despair. He clutched her to his chest, her blood soaking through his clothes as he rocked back and forth, whispering broken pleas. "Baby, please."

Mylan stood a few feet away, his own tears carving silent paths down his face. The sight of his baby sister, his fierce, resilient Nora, lying lifeless in Warren's arms was a punch to his gut, stealing the breath from his lungs.

The wail of sirens filled the air, echoing off the walls of the casino and signaling the arrival of the police and EMTs. The flashing lights painted the room in harsh, alternating hues of red and blue, illuminating the chaos that had just unfolded.

Uniformed officers rushed in, assessing the scene, while the EMTs moved swiftly to the center of the room, their stretchers and medical bags at the ready. They paused when they saw Nora, understanding immediately that there was nothing more to be done.

"Sir," one of the EMTs said gently, crouching down beside Warren. "We need to take her now."

Warren didn't seem to hear them at first, his body rocking as he clung to Nora. His tears fell onto her still face, and he brushed them away with trembling fingers, whispering words of love and apology.

Mylan watched from a few feet away, his own eyes filled with tears that he struggled to contain. He moved closer, kneeling beside Warren and placing a firm but gentle hand on his shoulder.

"It's okay," Mylan said, his voice thick with emotion. "She's okay now. You can let go."

Mylan offered Warren a hand to help him rise. Warren accepted it, though his legs felt weak and unsteady beneath him. Together, they watched as the EMTs wheeled Nora away, the world around them feeling strangely empty and quiet.

Warren turned away from the wreckage of the casino, knowing that the road ahead wouldn't be easy, but it would be worth it. He would carry Nora's spirit with him, a reminder of the strength they had shared and the love that would guide him toward a better future.

The End

Epilogue

A sign reading "Congratulations, Sage" hung prominently in the living room. Everyone had gathered at Paulette's apartment to celebrate. The room buzzed with laughter and conversation, a sense of warmth and healing permeating the air.

Mylan cradled baby Laverne, who had grown a little heavier over the past year and a half. He tossed her gently in the air, catching her with ease, both of them giggling in delight. His face showed signs of the grief he carried, but the love for his family was undeniable.

In the kitchen, Avery and Paulette worked together, carefully baking cupcakes. At 14, Avery had developed a keen interest in cooking, eagerly learning from Paulette. "One day, I'll open my own restaurant," Avery declared confidently as she mixed the batter.

Paulette smiled warmly, wiping her hands on her apron. "With your determination, there's no doubt about it," she replied, placing the cupcake tray into the oven.

Celine and Douglas engaged in a conversation, the atmosphere lightened by the festive mood around them. "So, what exactly do you do?" Douglas asked, a curious glint in his eye.

Celine shot him a playful side-eye. "Off the record?" she chuckled, taking a sip of her drink.

"Off the record," he assured her with a grin.

"I own a modeling agency," she said, a hint of laughter in her voice, knowing that she was lying.

Douglas leaned in, lowering his voice. "You should work for me at my private investigator firm," he suggested a twinkle of mischief in his eyes.

"What, finding missing girls?" Celine laughed, shaking her head.

"Yes, I can use your expertise," he said with a wink.

Celine raised an eyebrow, a smile tugging at the corners of her lips. "I'm not sure if my expertise extends to chasing down leads and staking out suspects."

Douglas chuckled, "You'd be surprised. You've got an eye for details, and that's half the job."

"Hmm," she mused, pretending to consider it. "Maybe I'll stick to runway shows and photo shoots. Less danger, more glamor."

Douglas nodded, a smirk on his face. "Well, if you ever get tired of the glamor, you know where to find me."

Celine laughed softly. "I'll keep that in mind."

Sage, Tegan, and Cylus sat on the couch, their voices buzzing with excitement about the future. "I can't believe you got into Westbridge University," Cylus said, grinning at Sage with pride.

Sage shrugged a modest smile on her face. "I worked hard for it. Plus, all those late-night study sessions paid off."

Tegan nodded excitedly. "I always knew you'd get in. You've got that drive, girl. And the basketball scholarship is just the cherry on top."

Cylus gave Sage a playful nudge. "You're gonna crush it there. Westbridge has no idea what's coming."

Sage laughed, feeling the warmth of their support. "Thanks, you guys. I just hope I can keep up with everything."

"Don't worry," Tegan assured her. "You've got us cheering for you every step of the way. And with Cylus already going to Westbridge, you've got a built-in support system."

Cylus nodded. "Yep, we're gonna take Westbridge by storm together."

Sage felt a wave of gratitude wash over her, knowing she had such good friends by her side. The future felt bright and full of possibilities, and she was ready to embrace it all.

Warren clicked a glass to get everyone's attention, his voice warm and full of pride. Everyone looked at him, their chatter subsiding as they focused on his words. "I just want to say congratulations to my daughter on her acceptance into Westbridge. We are all so proud of you and wish you nothing but the best," he announced, his eyes glistening with emotion.

Sage stood beside him, beaming. She embraced Warren tightly, feeling the strength of his love and support. "Thank you, everyone, for being here and supporting me when I was at my lowest. I wouldn't have made it without you all."

Avery walked over and wrapped her arms around Sage, pulling her into a warm hug. "I'm going to miss you, but I can't wait to get your room," she laughed, teasing her sister with a playful grin.

Sage chuckled, ruffling Avery's hair affectionately. "You better take good care of it," she replied, winking at her younger sister.

Sage's phone vibrated in her pocket, and she stepped into the hallway for some privacy. On the other end, an automated voice came through, "This is a collect call from Kamari Willis, an inmate at Brookstone Women's

Penitentiary. To accept this call, please press 1. To decline, please hang up. This call may be monitored or recorded for security purposes."

With a quick press of 1, Sage accepted the call. "Kamari," Sage said, the familiarity of the voice on the other end bringing a flood of memories.

"Hey, miss college student. Congratulations!" Kamari's voice carried a warmth Sage had almost forgotten.

Sage leaned against the wall, a smile tugged at her lips. "Thanks. I never thought I'd actually get into Westbridge."

Kamari chuckled softly. "Of course you did. You've got the brains and the grit. I am so proud of you, and I'm sure she is too." Kamari's voice softened, her words heavy with the unspoken presence of Nora.

Sage rubbed the pendant on her necklace, a cherished keepsake that had belonged to Nora. The cool metal seemed to hum with the warmth of her mother's spirit, grounding her in the moment. "Yeah, I know she is." Her voice wavered, emotions swirling beneath the surface. The pendant was more than a piece of jewelry; it was a link to her mother.

As the family gathered, there was an evident sense of hope and renewal in the air. With the darkness of the past finally lifting, they could look forward to a future filled with promise and possibility. They had weathered many storms, but their bonds were stronger than ever. With optimism and love, they were ready to embrace whatever the future held together.

www.ingramcontent.com/pod-product-compliance
Lightning Source LLC
Chambersburg PA
CBHW072130300726
48975CB00003B/999